THE LUSITANIA CONSPIRACY

THE LUSITANIA CONSPIRACY

A NOVEL

RONALD J. WALTERS

WALTERS MEDIA, LLC ~ TRAVERSE CITY, MICHIGAN

Published by
Walters Media, LLC
Traverse City, MI

Publisher's Cataloging-in-Publication Data
Walters, Ronald J.

The Lusitania conspiracy / Ronald J. Walters. – Traverse City, MI : Walters Media, LLC, 2015.

p. ; cm.

ISBN13: 978-0-9860846-0-7

1. Lusitania (Steamship)—Fiction. 2. Shipwrecks—History—20th century—Fiction. 3. World War, 1914-1918—Fiction. I. Title.

PS3623.A48 L8 2015
813.6—dc23 2015901840

Project coordination by Jenkins Group, Inc.
www.BookPublishing.com

Interior design by Brooke Camfield

Printed in the United States of America

19 18 17 16 15 • 5 4 3 2 1

Dedication

This book is dedicated to my mother, Frances Walters, who passed onto me her love of reading. Some of my earliest memories are of sitting in my parents' living room prior to kindergarten with my mother reading in her chair and me reading the *World Book Encyclopedia*, volume by volume. I have always been fascinated by facts. Each time I finished a volume my mother would ask me what I learned. Before I started school I had read every volume. Of course my retention was minimal at four and five years of age, but I did always take something away from each book, especially volume D; that's where the Dinosaurs lived.

My mother was voracious at solving crossword puzzles. I also picked up this habit. As the youngest of ten children born to chicken farmers, I saw what many years of hard thankless work can do to a person. My mother looked old beyond her time and had little joy in her life. Books, the newspaper, and the Bible were her escape. I wish she could have lived to read this. Not heavy on praise, she probably would have said something to the effect of "if you like that sort of thing I guess it was somewhat entertaining," but inside she would have been smiling.

I would also like to dedicate this book to my sister Joan, whose unwavering support of me in all my endeavors has been a constant throughout my life.

Most of what you are about to read is true.
Well . . . a lot of it, anyway.
The rest is just wild fun.

Contents

PROLOGUE: COVER-UP

In the Celtic Sea, less than twelve miles off the coast of Ireland, due south of a craggy, windswept lonely spit of land known as Old Head of Kinsale, lay the wreck.

It was September 1948: thirty-three years after the sinking, thirty years after the end of World War I (the so-called war to end all wars), and three years after the world war that had followed.

For decades people had known, of course, that the ship was down there, somewhere. But it had taken Britain most of those decades to recover from two nearly consecutive world wars and then to construct a vessel capable of reaching the wreck. That vessel was the HMS *Reclaim*, now anchored 295 murky feet above the site.

Barely six months old and not yet officially commissioned by the British Royal Navy, this was the *Reclaim*'s shakedown cruise, her first mission, her raison d'être. She had been built for one purpose only: deep diving and submarine rescue—the Royal Navy's first and only such ship. This operation, classified "Above Top Secret," was off-book. It had to be because the *Reclaim* wasn't anchored in the cold waters off the rugged coast of Ireland that fall day to perform a rescue. She was there to cover up a war crime against humanity.

And to help commit murder.

* * *

On the rolling deck of the HMS *Reclaim*, two officers—the commander, heavyset, with full beard, ruddy face, and intense eyes, and a US Navy captain, younger, compact, with a dark moustache—peered into the dark, choppy waters beneath the arm of a swing crane jutting over the side of the ship.

A young, Royal Navy seaman operated the crane, its taut steel cables snaking up and around the pulley and down into the inky water below. A grizzled, older chief petty officer guided air hoses as they slowly unrolled from large spools and fed over the side of the ship. A diesel engine–powered air pump droned steadily on the deck next to the chief.

The chief petty officer and the seaman labored in tandem, carefully coordinating the movements of the swing-arm and the crane with the choppy swells of the roiling ocean.

Black thunderclouds were gathering across the steel sky. A large wave suddenly slammed into the side of the boat. Air hoses and cables whipped violently.

The seaman flinched, his grip momentarily slipping from the controls.

The commander glanced at him sharply.

"Steady, *steady*, Seaman!" the chief petty officer growled at the seaman.

"Aye, Chief. Sorry, Chief," the seaman said nervously, doubling his grip on the control panel.

The chief leaned down and tapped the glass facing of the air pressure gauge on the air pump. The needle fluttered in a steady rhythm as air fed into the hoses. He raised his sleeve, looked at his watch, and turned to the commander.

"Near forty-five minutes down, sir."

"I can tell time, Chief," the commander replied gruffly. "Just keep pumping good air down and foul air up."

"Aye, sir."

The US Navy captain turned to the commander and said, "How long can they stay down?"

The commander glanced at his watch and responded, "Less than one hour more." He looked out at the blackening sky. "I'm more worried about us than them. We must get moving. If this weather keeps up, we'll be taking lightning."

The commander nodded down at the dense, gray water and added, "The only safe place then will be down there, with them." He thought a moment and added under his breath, "Though not for long, I'm afraid."

Two hundred and ninety five feet below the *Reclaim*, on the deck of the RMS *Lusitania*, two bronze-helmeted divers in lead boots and oiled canvas diving suits were making their way slowly, one behind the other, across the debris-strewn, mangled deck of the once magnificent "Greyhound of the Sea," now listing toward her starboard side.

Their dim-wattage torches swept back and forth in front of them, their air hoses snaking from the top of their brass helmets like antennas, disappearing up into the murky waters to the *Reclaim* above.

"Twelve hundred souls she took down," the lead diver said into his microphone.

The divers stopped and solemnly looked around the wreck.

The second diver said, "Kaiser Wilhelm's U-boat took them down, you mean."

As the divers slowly made their way across the slanted deck, their leaden boots kicked up fine silt, revealing thousands of rifle cartridges and hundreds of empty shell casings strewn about.

The lead diver reached down and scooped up a handful of the corroded shells. He slid a few into a pocket of his suit, turned to the other diver, and held one up.

"Three ought threes, these are. Same as we got at Gallipoli in '15. Jammers these bloody things were. Don't know why they expected anything but what we got from the Turks in that one."

The second diver abruptly stopped working and looked at him in awe.

"You're saying . . . *you* were at the Dardanelles?"

The lead diver's helmet bobbed. "That I was, son. And these things damn near got me killed."

"Bloody hell," the second diver said reverently. "Most honored to be in your company, sir. Most honored."

The lead diver stopped suddenly as his light beam captured a ghostly object sitting on the ocean floor a short distance away from the nearly 800-foot ship: a hulking, barnacle-covered device, barely visible under years of decay, a cross between a cannon-shaped "ray gun" and a two-pronged tuning fork.

"The board," he said to the diver behind him.

The second diver held up a writing slate on which a technical drawing had been made. He aimed his torch at it. The lead diver moved his light from the drawing, back to the device, and to the drawing again, comparing the two. They were the same.

"That's it," the lead diver said.

Topside, on the *Reclaim*, a red light on a bulky black phone on the air pump began flashing. The chief grabbed the phone, put it to his ear, strained to hear.

"Say again?"

The commander reached out a hand. "I'll take that, Chief."

"Aye, sir."

The chief handed him the phone. The commander, too, strained to hear.

"Repeat yourself, Seaman," he said into the phone. "And speak loudly."

"We've found it, sir," came the tinny voice of the lead diver over the phone.

The commander's expression changed.

"Say again—you've found it? Is that affirmative?"

"Affirmative, sir. I'm looking at it right now, Commander. It seems to be intact. Tidal currents are pretty strong down here. Lots of sediment kicking up. Dim visibility. None too stable . . . But it's here, all right."

Down on the *Lusitania*, the second diver asked the lead diver, "What the devil is it? Why send us down after three decades to salvage this, this . . . *what is it*, anyway?"

"What it is, gentlemen," came the voice of the commander over their helmet speakers, "is *nonexistent*. Now report: how bad is the damage to the ship's magazine area—have you seen it?"

"Just passed the magazine, Commander. No damage at all, just a lot of shell casings and cartridges. Couple broken cases of fuses."

"Torpedo holes in the starboard hull—how many?"

"She's listing to starboard, sir. Too tight to get down there to see. No real visibility even if we could. No explosion damage on the port side, though."

"Very well. Prepare the device for salvage. A storm is on us up here."

"Aye, sir."

The divers set about securing the contraption and attaching cables to it.

Above the wreck, the storm was intensifying. The commander handed the phone back to the chief and looked at the American.

"They're on the *Lusitania*," he said. "They've found the Tesla device nearby."

The American turned, gripped the rail with both hands, and peered anxiously down into the black water.

"By God," he said. "What would Tesla say, were he still alive?"

The commander responded, "I wonder if the damn thing still works."

The winch groaned and the swing-arm cable stretched taut as the odd looking device, covered in a dripping tarp that was bound by straps, slowly broke the choppy surface of the water. The crane swiveled it over the deck. Crewmen guided it over the gaping hold.

The American stared intently at the odd-shaped device as it was slowly lowered down into the bowels of the ship.

The commander turned to the American and said, "Now that Britain has entertained what is certain to be your country's next folly, Captain, I must complete my . . . *depth charge exercise*."

"From a submarine rescue vessel, no less," the American added to the commander's statement. "The irony does not escape me, Commander. We all have our secrets. Do what you must."

Suddenly, jagged fingers of lightning raked across the darkening firmament, followed by the crashing boom of thunder. The rain pummeling the tarp-wrapped device as it settled onto the bottom of the hold exploded like little balls of electric light dancing in the pulsing storm.

The commander turned to the chief petty officer.

"It's time, Chief." He paused. "Take the boys home."

The chief looked at the commander a moment, nodded, and looked down at the deck. "Aye, Commander."

The chief squatted down next to the diesel pump. He hesitated a second. He shut off the air valve and killed the motor.

Down on the *Lusitania*, the lead diver suddenly clutched at his helmet, his face contorted grotesquely, mouth gasping, eyes bulging.

The second diver approached him in alarm.

"What is it, mate!?"—then he too suddenly began gasping, his hands beating at the glass in his faceplate.

The lead diver caved to his knees. His suit began collapsing in on him, the compression squeezing his body up into his helmet.

The second diver's suit began imploding as well. The men screamed in agony. Their helmets filled with blood . . . and exploded in a silent, red mist.

Up on the deck of the *Reclaim*, pelting rain and hurricane-force wind was lashing at the ship.

The chief petty officer stood, looked at the commander, and gave a slight nod.

"They're home, sir," he said quietly.

The commander nodded. He turned to the American. The two men's eyes locked.

"As you said, Captain, we all have secrets. And they *will* be kept."

"Then I trust you'll be as efficient at tying off the Bletchley team—whose code breaking put them in the *know* about what happened—as you were those poor sods down there, Commander."

The commander looked at him sharply. "Are you mad, Captain? The group at Bletchley can *keep* a secret—hell, their code breaking revealed those two!" He composed himself, then added, "We picked those divers because Bletchley discovered certain weaknesses in their patriotic fervor. Particularly the lead diver. His politics had shifted considerably by the time he returned home from Gallipoli in 1915. We kept him in the service because we thought he might come in handy. And so he has."

The American looked down into the hold as the steel doors grinded shut against the pelting rain.

"And what about the younger fellow, Commander? Was he simply *expendable*?"

"We did what we had to, Captain. Perhaps espionage is the wrong business for you to be in if you find the necessities of war so objectionable."

The commander turned abruptly and barked orders at the chief. "Prepare to drop charges. Tell the con, all ahead full, circle wide, starboard tack."

"Aye, sir."

The massive turbines of the HMS *Reclaim* thundered to full throttle. The ship cut a wide swath around the site as depth charges were dropped. Moments later, huge explosions sent geysers of water gushing toward the stormy sky.

The heavens answered with a bolt of lightning that tore across the Celtic Sea . . . forever burning the stormy image of their crimes into the memories of the men who had committed them.

CHAPTER 1

Child of Light

One dark and rainy afternoon in 1909, Nikola Tesla, Serbian electrical and mechanical engineer, inventor and futurist, stood alone in the center of an open field in lower Manhattan as the heavens deluged him with cracking thunder and lightning—tumultuous events that seemed to follow Tesla wherever he went, even when not produced by Mother Nature.

His long, black waistcoat whipped against the wind as blinding, jagged bolts of lightning tore through the rain, exploding in showering displays of sparks, crashing near him.

Tesla, standing six feet, two inches tall and weighing 150 pounds, cut a tranquil and stylish figure in the middle of the angry elements that were seemingly threatening to destroy him. His blue eyes, intently scrutinizing the magnificent demonstration, barely squinted as the blinding flashes lit up his face. Occasionally, Tesla would stroke his dark, elegant moustache as he calmly studied the conflagration swirling about him, lighting up the building behind him as if by the noonday sun.

* * *

Nikola Tesla had been born, more than five decades earlier, at midnight on July 10, 1856, in a tiny bedroom in the small, Serbian village of Smiljan during a similar and equally fierce electrical storm.

That night, crashing thunder shook the little house, startling the midwife as she laid the infant into the outstretched arms of his mother, lying on the bed. Tesla's mother, Đuka, daughter of an Orthodox priest, took the little boy to her bosom and tenderly pulled the bedspread over them both.

The midwife stepped back from the bed and glanced fearfully at the blackness beyond the rain soaked windowpane.

"*To je loš znak*," (This is a bad omen.) she uttered, wringing her hands.

"*Ovo dete će biti dete tame*," (This child will be a child of darkness.) she added in a whisper.

Just then, a crack of lightning tore open the night sky outside, brightening the room as if a flaming comet had swept past the window, revealing the radiant smile of the young mother as she looked into the face of her little newborn.

"*Ne*," (No) Đuka Tesla said, smiling as she gently cradled young Nikola in her arms. "*On će biti dete svetlosti*." (He will be a child of light.)

And so he had become.

* * *

Fifty-three years later Nikola Tesla was standing in a Manhattan field in the middle of an electrical storm, sixty feet away from a twenty-foot-high pole, on top of which was mounted a large brass ball. Several wires ran down the pole and into a cylindrical core that looked like a large, round, lion cage. Tesla's eyes absorbed the increasing intensity of the scene, his mind computing and analyzing. A bolt of lightning suddenly struck the pole. The core sparked to life. A glass tube flashed blue-white. The core exploded. Another flash of lightning struck telephone wires across the road, causing them to vibrate, hum, and pulse, with increasing intensity, all the way to a transformer on another pole. The transformer vibrated violently and suddenly exploded in a blinding shower of electricity.

Tesla turned suddenly and rushed to the building behind him. He shouldered the door open and burst inside, into a spacious, high-ceilinged, well-organized scientific laboratory.

"Li! Li!" he shouted excitedly, peeling off his sopping wet coat.

He draped his coat on a rack by the door and dashed to a large chalkboard mounted on a wall. He grabbed a piece of chalk and scrawled on the board in big letters:

FOCUS!

He underlined the word several times.

"Li! Where the devil are you, man?!"

A roof access door was flung open and a young Chinese man half Tesla's age scrambled inside, slammed the door behind him, and padded quickly down the staircase.

"Yes, Boss! You okay—did it take the charge?"

Tesla whirled on Li, pulled him close by the lapels, eyes wild with excitement, and said, "Focus!" He lowered his voice to a near whisper and repeated, "It's about focus, Li. Fo-cus, my man."

"I am focused, Boss. What you got?"

"We focus the vibration to its natural resonance."

"We do?"

"Yes. We do. Then we isolate the individual tone—the unique oscillation that makes up, well, *everything*, *everyone*. Each oscillatory tone is unique, they're all different, no two are alike, you have your unique tonal oscillation that makes up *you* as human being, I do—even rocks do. Are you following me, Li?"

"Yes, Boss, yes, following, following. What next?"

"Isolating the individual tone releases the energy trapped inside—the energy that creates the tone, the resonance. It doubles, quadruples, octuples, and so forth, and by using the harmonic convergences of several different frequencies in tandem, it increases the combined energy and its corresponding power exponentially. You understand me, Li? It's not that dissimilar to the concept of a boy using a magnifying lens to focus the sun's light on an ant and popping its—here, let me show you."

Tesla stopped mid-sentence, pressed Li aside, franticly searched a lab table, grabbed a toaster-sized object, and held it up like a prize trophy.

"This oscillator is the key—our 'magnifying lens of energy,' so to speak. Are you getting this?"

Li's eyes lit up. "Yes, yes—your resonance oscillator, Boss. But,"—he jabbed a finger at a dented cylindrical device on the table and said, "the core—was it damaged?"

"Yes, but—no, actually it just needs a little more work, some fine-tuning."

Tesla, eyes darting, mind spinning, was a whirling dervish.

"Fetch me the level!"

"Yes, Boss!"

Li started to dash away. Tesla grabbed him by the arm and said, "And *focus*, man! Focus!"

"I am focused, Boss."

"Good. Go!"

Li trotted quickly away.

"And the big clamps!" Tesla called out after him. "Quickly!—we cannot lose the storm!"

"Yes, Boss!"

"And the battery! Get the battery, too!"

"Focusing on the battery, Boss. And the big clamps! And the level!"

Tesla grabbed the oscillator, ran to the door, grabbed a rain slicker off the rack.

"Boss," Li called out as he grabbed the items and stuffed them into a deep duffel bag. "Don't forget dinner."

Tesla called over his shoulder as he grabbed the door handle, "I'm not hungry, Li! We have work to do!"

"Are you forgetting?"

Tesla stopped, turned. "Forgetting what, Li? What am I forgetting? We have the clamps, we have the batt—"

"No, Boss," Li said, trotting over to him, lugging a large duffel bag. "Dinner, Boss."

"Dinner? This is hardly the time for dinner, Li. I'm not even hungry."

"But you had dinner plans with Mr. Twai—"

Tesla whipped open the door—and was momentarily taken aback at the sight of Mark Twain standing there, dressed all in white, his fist poised to knock, umbrella held aloft in the other hand, and sweeping white moustache dripping.

"Ah!—perfect timing, Nicky," Twain said and smiled.

He began closing his umbrella as he stepped past Tesla into the room.

Li stopped behind Tesla and gave a knowing smile to Twain.

Twain stopped rolling his umbrella and looked from Tesla to Li and back.

"What?" Twain asked.

Li reached out and took Twain's umbrella.

Twain looked at the oscillator in Tesla's arms, tugged thoughtfully at the end of his moustache, and asked with a raised eyebrow, "Would I be wrong to assume that our plans have changed?"

Tesla grinned, hefted the oscillator into Twain's arms, and pulled him into an awkward embrace.

"*Improved* would be a better word," Tesla said. "Our plans have improved, my dear Twain, by a fortuitous happenstance of nature. You will earn your meal tonight, my good friend!"

"Then let's work up an appetite," Twain responded cheerfully, sheltering the heavy oscillator in the crook of his arm while Tesla adjusted the umbrella to cover the device.

"I would also bet a Delmonico's rib eye steak and a glass of Kentucky bourbon that the great Nikola Tesla is on the verge of another world-shattering discovery."

Li swung open the door. Rain and wind rushed in.

Tesla shouted at Twain over the cacophony, "In a good way! Always in a good way!"

The two friends plowed gleefully headfirst into the dark storm. Li followed, slamming the door behind him.

As the trio ran, the image of their bent backs and running legs was momentarily frozen in a *CRAAACK* of biblical-sized lightning.

CHAPTER 2

The Carnage Beyond the Fence

Tesla, Twain, and Li splashed through puddles, winding their way through the narrow, cobblestone streets of a derelict lower Manhattan neighborhood.

An angry *A-OOOO-GA*! blared as Tesla nearly became the hood ornament of a Talbot Clement a half second before Twain yanked him safely out of its way.

The three men stopped and huddled together in an alcove, hearts pounding madly, catching their breath as the Talbot roared down the rainy road.

Twain patted Li on the back, called to Tesla over the pouring rain, "What mischief have you dragged your poor coolie into this time, Nicky?"

Li eyed Twain indignantly. "*Coolie?*" he said. "You know what coolie means, Mr. Mark Twain?"

Nervously, Twain replied, "Why, yes, it's a, that would be a, er—"

"Low paid dock worker!" Li announced sullenly. "I'm not low paid."

"Ah, but you do work for a doc," Twain grinned, nodding toward Tesla.

"Oh, now you're a comedian," Li scoffed.

"My 'mischief,' dear Twain," Tesla said, "is a most amazing experiment indeed."

He suddenly bolted down the road. Twain and Li trotted after him.

Li, panting and heaving, hands on knees, canvas bag slung over his back, stammered, "B-Boss, you run too fast. G-get us all killed."

A few minutes later, they reached their destination: a fenced off, abandoned, half-finished structure with a hand-printed warning sign hanging on the fence.

DANGER: CONSTRUCTION SITE!

Authorized Personal Only!

Trespassers Will Be Persecuted!

Twain chuckled as he read the crude misspellings.

"I'm not sure how they mean to *persecute* us," Twain said. His eyes fell on Li, who was cutting through the fence with wire cutters. "Now, that'll get us persecuted *and* prosecuted, by golly."

"Nothing personal," Li said as a gap appeared in the fencing and the warning sign clattered to the ground.

They stepped through the opening and made their way to the rusting skeleton of the building ahead.

Tesla examined the riveted metal I-beams. “Li,” he said, pointing to a particular I-beam. “Right here—we’ll put it here.”

“Right, Boss.”

Li took the oscillator from Twain and handed it to Tesla. Tesla pressed it against various places on the rusted beams.

“This is a lot of steel,” Twain remarked, looking up at thirty feet of massive steel girders silhouetted in the pattering rain.

Li pulled a large level from the canvas bag, lifted it to the front of a metal archway, and clamped it across the opening.

Twain looked at Tesla, puzzled, and asked, “What is that for?”

“Perfect way to measure movement,” Tesla answered as he attached the oscillator to the base of a structural beam.

“Oh, well that explains that,” Twain deadpanned.

“Everything is made up of moving atoms,” Tesla explained. “It is this constant motion of atoms at particular frequencies, this inertia,that creates mass—a body, a structure, a stone, even water. They all have mass, which is created from tiny, moving, atom particles. Everything in nature vibrates at its own particular frequency. Velocity creates density, mass. When an object oscillates at it’s own exact resonance, it exponentially compounds itself until a shock wave encompasses the entire structure, rendering it malleable.”

“But that compounded resonance creates friction, doesn’t it?” Twain asked.

“Precisely—which is why the mass becomes malleable.”

“But Nicky, three stories’ worth of steel beams becoming malleable, as in moving or, dare I say it, melting? Won’t that be dangerous?”

“Only if we’re successful,” Tesla said and nodded.

Tesla attached a red wire to a nickel-iron car battery bearing a nameplate *Edison Battery.*

"The only thing direct current is good for," Tesla said disdainfully as he wrapped the wire around the post on the battery. He chuckled and added, "If we're successful, I might just leave this battery here and have that bastard Edison take the blame."

"Blame?" Twain said nervously. "Blame for what, Nicky? What are you going to do?"

Tesla grinned at Twain and said, "You'll see. Watch the bubbles. They dance." He nodded at Li and Twain and announced, "Gentlemen, stand clear."

Tesla flipped a switch. The oscillator hummed to life, shooting roaring vibrations up the metal beams.

"Look!" Li said excitedly, pointing at the structure. "It's moving!"

Tesla looked up, exhilarated. Li placed a hand delicately on a vibrating beam. Twain looked as if he were about to pass out from fear.

"It's singing," Tesla yelled at Twain over the loudening hum. "Can you hear it?"

"Oh, I hear it, all right!" Twain yelled back. "I just hope it's not *Lord, I'm Coming Home!*"

The hum reached a piercing pitch. The sound of glass shattering emanated from the building. The beams themselves seemed to squeal and shriek.

"Nicky! Is this normal?!" Twain yelled over the fray. "Why is it doing this?!"

"Because it's reciprocating electricity in on itself, from the resonant oscillations!"

"Thank you. Your explanations are as clear as Mississippi mud. And I'm too old for this. May we go to dinner, please?"

Suddenly, there was an ominous moaning sound of twisting, buckling steel.

The trio instinctively backed away, watching in open-mouthed amazement as the structure began to contort like a giant pretzel. Rivets began to pop from joints, sending one smashing through the cab of a steam shovel. The sounds increased, like something from a war zone, with rivets ricocheting off steel beams like bullets.

Tesla, Twain, and Li scampered behind a pile of bricks. Twain's eyes were wide with amazement. Tesla was grinning like a schoolboy throwing firecrackers in the girl's bathroom.

"Like Chinese New Year!" Li cried out in glee.

"I think we've had enough, boys!" Twain yelled.

Tesla stood and moved toward the oscillator. Far above, metal was tearing with ungodly groaning. Suddenly, a tree-trunk-sized I-beam angled down and plummeted like a giant arrow toward him. Li leapt up and threw himself in a perfect spiral into the space in front of Tesla, expertly shoving Tesla and Twain clear and tucking out of the way just as the torn beam embedded itself into the ground with a loud, quivering thud in the exact space where they had stood a half a second earlier.

Li deftly recovered and jumped to his feet, with the oscillator in his hands.

Disconnected from the battery, the device powered down, and the humming sound faded and died. With one last shivering vibration, the building went still and silent.

Unsteadily, Tesla stood.

The building looked as if God had pinched it between his fingers.

"Li," Tesla said, looking at his faithful assistant. "Remind me to give you a raise."

"Th-that's quite a weapon you've got there," Twain exclaimed nervously, still lying on the ground trying to catch his breath.

"Weapon?" Tesla replied. "No, not—not a *weapon*, Twain. Not at all. Imagine using this to explore, to dig, to render the earth malleable, to move massive objects out of the way in a construction site, for example, to build homes. Laborers will be more productive and protected. My goal—my life's work—is to make this new century more humane. A century for the people."

"Mr. Tesla," Twain said deferentially. "Your resonance oscillator is a weapon. Ever since a caveman first picked up a stick or Cain slew Abel. It is human nature, my friend. You have created the most powerful weapon known to man. Now, help an old man up, if you will."

Tesla reached down and helped pull Twain to his feet. Twain was clearly in discomfort, straining to breath.

"Are you all right, my friend?" Tesla asked, concern on his face as Twain stood shakily.

"Just . . . just let me catch my breath," Twain responded, rubbing his sternum.

"I shouldn't have brought you," Tesla exclaimed.

"Oh, stop it. If it wasn't for you, Nicky, I'd have died after I lost Olivia five years ago. I've had more fun with you than with anyone in my life."

The two men shared a glance.

"I know your mother was taken from you, as well," Tesla said quietly.

"Death takes us all, eventually," Twain replied.

"Only to begin the next adventure I have in store for you, my dear friend," Tesla responded.

"Ha! You are a bit of a mad scientist, Nicky," Twain said. "But I don't doubt your mind could conjure up such a feat. No doubt at all."

They looked at each other a serious moment. They embraced.

Twain said, his eyes misty, "I came into Earth with Halley's Comet, as is well known. It is scheduled to pass by again next year, my friend. And I expect to go out with it. For I have no doubt the Almighty once said: *Now here are these two unaccountable freaks; they came in together, they must go out together*."

"*Freaks*?" Tesla asked suspiciously. "Which two freaks are you referring to, my dear Twain?"

Suddenly, a wailing police siren blared from down the road. The three men spun about looking in the direction of the gate.

"RUN!" Tesla shouted.

Tesla took Twain by the arm. Twain threw down his now-shredded umbrella. With Li in the lead, the three men bolted into the darkness like school chums caught toilet-papering the principal's house at midnight.

With screaming sirens closing in on the construction site, they vanished around a corner and clattered down the road. A man's face glowed briefly from the shadows, illuminated as he applied the small flame from his gold lighter to a cigarette. He stepped from the shadows, watching the three escape.

He calmly sauntered off in their direction, disappearing just as three NYPD squad cars screeched up to the gate, their pulsing cherries pumping a ghoulish red glow over the carnage beyond the fence.

CHAPTER 3

WORLD ON FIRE

Over the next sixty months, Nikola Tesla, widely acknowledged as possessing one of the greatest scientific minds in history, would be tested like no other period in his life.

After successfully destroying the steel frame of the unfinished building near his Manhattan lab, Tesla continued perfecting his harmonic oscillator. From his work on ever-evolving iterations of the oscillator, Tesla was able to unravel the mystery of the relationship of electricity and gravity.

Li, who was no mental slouch himself, often felt he was left in Tesla's dust and did his best to keep up with Tesla's racing mind.

"Sometimes you remind me of Albert," Li once had quipped to his stylishly dressed, fashion-plate boss in reference to Albert Einstein. "And other times you're more like Sherlock Holmes."

Li chuckled and added, "If those two had a kid together, it would be you, Boss!"

Tesla stopped what he was doing, turned down the flame on his blowtorch, looked at Li over the rims of his dark welding glasses, and retorted, "And what do you know about Albert Einstein that would make you think he'd have . . . *relations* with Sherlock Holmes?"

"It was a joke, Boss," Li answered sheepishly.

"In that case, Li, work on your routine," Tesla responded, shaking his head and pointing to a pair of stainless steel forceps on the lab bench. "And hand me those forceps."

Tesla picked a microscopic piece of lint from his lab coat, turned up the flame on the torch, took the forceps from Li, and resumed working on the harmonic oscillator.

Meticulous in grooming and clothing, and with an almost regal bearing—complete with a lightly imperious air—Nikola Tesla cut an elegant figure around New York City, catching the eye of many a young lady who was attracted as much to his handsome features as to the fact that he was an incredibly wealthy man.

But women did not fit into Tesla's demanding and precise routine. He felt their need for time and attention cheated him of time from his beloved pursuits of scientific discovery. It would take a truly special woman to catch the eye of Nikola Tesla.

Highly regimented in his activities, Tesla followed a precise routine and was very set in his habits. Li had learned this early on, from way back when Tesla had won him from Mark Twain in a game of rotation. By the time Twain had chalked his 21-weight cue stick and was blowing blue dust from the felt tip, Tesla had run the entire table.

Li could set his watch by Tesla. Better still, with Tesla around, Li didn't need a watch. Tesla walked every day, sun or rain. A brisk walk four or five miles out, and four or five back. Li knew when it was precisely 6:10 in the evening, by three words Tesla would call out.

"Li! Let's walk."

Li enjoyed these vigorously paced walks with his enigmatic and energetic boss, because during these times they discussed various experiments, unpacked and solved different scientific challenges, and "divined and solved the world," as Tesla put it.

Tesla worked every day from nine in the morning until six in the evening. He ate dinner at exactly ten past eight, usually at Delmonico's restaurant or at the Waldorf-Astoria Hotel, where he and Li lived. After dinner, he would resume his work until two or three in the morning. This routine, of course, drove the indomitable Li up a freaking wall. But the ever-faithful assistant was not merely devoted to Tesla; he darn near idolized the man—though he was careful not to display his devotion.

Tesla devoured various scientific works, memorized complete books, utilizing his eidetic memory. Merely by hearing the name of an idea or invention in his mind, he was able to instantly visualize it in full color, with extreme precision, including minute dimensions. From this "mental blueprint," he was then able to move on to the construction stage and build—entirely from memory—the device he had created in his mind.

Li was particularly intrigued about Tesla's work in focused magnetic resonance and electromagnetic fields, the backbone of the oscillator they were continually refining in the lab. Tesla had discovered that human beings were made up of photons—essentially, light itself—and that the unique individual oscillation that was the essence of each person did not end at physical death, but merely shifted the movements of their combination of photons, making them appear in a different physiological configuration—or not visible at all, although still present in another form.

As Li's mind attempted to knit together this barely comprehensible description of eternal life (basically), he deduced that Tesla's discovery may have had to do with the fact that he occasionally caught Tesla talking to . . . *nobody*—and animatedly, too, as if there *was* somebody standing right there with him. Li thought that either Tesla had figured out a way to actually see and converse with those who had, well, *passed on*, or he was a raving madman—who could rave in Serbo-Croatian, Czech, English, French, German, Hungarian, Italian, and Latin.

Explaining his theory at an eastern European symposium of scientists and physicists, Tesla had once put it this way: "*Ljudska svest menjaće granice života. To će biti moguće razgovarati sa dušama mrtvih.*" (Human consciousness will shift the boundaries of life . . . it will be possible to speak to the souls of the dead.)

One thing was sure: his theory (though not at all understood by his contemporaries) would come in very handy as 1909 gave way to the tragedy that was coming in 1910.

* * *

For some twenty years, Mark Twain had been a constant source of encouragement to Nikola Tesla. Twain had always been fascinated with science and had developed a close friendship with Tesla, spending time with the scientist in his laboratory, allowing himself to be photographed while indulging in some of Tesla's electrical experiments, causing Twain's famous mane of white hair to stand straight up as he gripped various electric devices in different stages of development.

Twain had been born around the same time Halley's Comet had flown past Earth, and he had once predicted that he would fly away with the comet when he died.

On April 21, 1910, Twain's prediction came true.

Upon hearing of Mark Twain's death, President William Howard Taft remarked, "Mark Twain gave pleasure, real intellectual enjoyment, to millions. His works will continue to give such pleasure to millions yet to come."

The president's last sentence was true concerning Twain's books and stories. But, to Tesla, it was true in another sense as well. For, while Twain had physically died, the atomic photon particles that made up Mark Twain as the world had known him had merely shifted onto a higher plane and reconstituted in an advanced dimension and in a form of physicality that only men with a mind like that of Nikola Tesla could conceive.

So, was Twain "dead"? No. Not really. At least not in the way the vast majority of people perceive the concept of death. Because, in Tesla's way of thinking, death itself could not kill a person's "life light"—particularly not a person such as Mark Twain.

Tesla and Li attended Twain's funeral at the Old Brick Presbyterian Church in New York City. He was laid to rest at Woodlawn Cemetery in Elmira, New York.

After the funeral service, they bid adieu to his daughter Clara, and gave their regards to various members of the Clemens family.

As they left the funeral, Tesla looked up into the blue sky and said to Li, "Isn't it interesting, Li, that Twain happened to have left Earth just one day after Halley's comet flew by the planet, precisely as he had predicted?"

Li nodded. They continued walking.

"I believe," Tesla continued, "that Halley picked up our friend . . . and blasted him into his next cosmic adventure."

Li looked up into the sky and smiled at the thought.

"He was a good man, Boss. Just like you."

Tesla hailed a taxi, and they headed back to the lab.

"Don't you find it fascinating, Li," Tesla remarked to Li as the cab bumped along the cobblestones, "that some people prefer to be buried when they die, whereas, others prefer . . . you know, to be . . ."

"Cremated, Boss?"

"Precisely. It doesn't really matter in the cosmic sense whether we are burned or buried. We are not our physicality on Earth, you know. We are only the visual representation of our essence. That is, how we are inside—our heart, our mind, our *spirit*—is how we are perceived by others on the outside."

"Uhhh . . . sure, right, Boss."

"But burning up the outside, that is, cremating the body, doesn't change the photonic makeup of our essence. Ashes or decaying bodies, Li, we are still who we always were before we died in this physical dimension. We are merely seen in a different light so to speak—at least to those who possess the imagination needed to see past the physical and to the spiritual." He looked at Li and asked, "Are you getting all this, Li?"

"Umm . . . right, Boss. Whatever you say. But, Boss?"

"Yes, Li?"

"Does all that mean you won't miss him?"

Tesla looked out the window pensively.

After a pause, he replied quietly, "Of course I will miss him. Tremendously. He *got* me." He looked at Li and added, "And that's precisely what I shall tell him when next I see him."

He rapped on the seat back in front of him and said, "Driver! Right side, on the corner. We're here."

It would be awhile before Tesla would see Mark Twain again. Until then, Tesla did what he did best. He buried himself in his work.

Though he was prone to secluding himself in his lab experiments, Tesla's reputation for being somewhat asocial stemmed from the fact that his patience tended to run thin around idiots. Fortunately, however, his mother Đuka had taught him an important skill as a child, one that had little to do with intellect.

"The definition of *tact*," Đuka had told young Nikola after he had tried to explain to one too many boys at school how dimwitted they were, "is how to tell someone to go to hell in such a way that they look forward to the trip."

He developed tact to a near science, and his social life soared.

Although he was a complex, engaging, and contemplative scientist, over the years Tesla developed into a true Renaissance man. He could be just as much a recluse as he could be the life of the party, often engaging in vibrant social activities, and counting many famous people among his friends. Not merely a scientist and engineer, he was also a poet and a philosopher, he loved classical music, he enjoyed fine food and good drink, and he particularly liked hitting the billiard tables, a game that was all math and angles, trajectory and inertia.

* * *

On June 28, 1914, Tesla was horrified at the somber news that five of his fellow Serbians, along with a man from Bosnia, had shot and killed Archduke Franz Ferdinand of Austria, heir to the Austro-Hungarian throne, and his wife, Sophie, Duchess of Hohenberg, while on a visit to Sarajevo, Bosnia.

Tesla stopped eating, pushed his dinner plate away from him slowly, shifted the newspaper front and center, and continued reading the terrible news.

The goal of the murders had been purely political: to force a separation of the south-Slavic provinces of Austria-Hungary and combine them into a Yugoslavia. Repercussions were nearly instantaneous. Austria-Hungary issued an ultimatum against Serbia to back off immediately. It was rejected.

After the Russian military came out in support of the Serbs, Austria-Hungary asked for Germany's help in attacking Serbia. Germany agreed, and on July 28, Austria-Hungary declared war on Serbia—and Russia immediately began mobilizing troops to defend them.

The dominoes began toppling.

Germany positioned itself on the side of Austria-Hungary and then formally declared war on Russia; signed a secret treaty with the Ottoman Empire; marched troops, tanks, and mortars into Luxemburg; and then declared war on France. Belgium refused to allow the German Army to cut through their country to go after France, so Germany invaded Belgium. On August 4, Great Britain dipped a toe into the fray by protesting the violation of Belgian neutrality. The German chancellor scoffed at the treaty, and Britain declared war on Germany.

By the middle of August, Europe was on fire, with Montenegro declaring war against Germany, France declaring war against Austria-Hungary, and the UK declaring war against Austria-Hungary.

* * *

In the meantime, as the winter of 1914 mired Europe down in a massive "war to end all wars," Nikola Tesla's Wardenclyffe tower, the wireless telecommunications facility he had built from 1901 to 1903 near Shoreham, Long Island with a loan from billionaire banker J. Pierpont Morgan, was suffering huge financial losses.

Prior to the start of the war, Tesla had sought overseas investors. But the European war had virtually eliminated the income he had been receiving from his patents in European countries. The pressure was on to consider selling off Wardenclyffe in order to continue funding his experiments and developing his electro-mechanical inventions.

Times had become desperate. Tesla was forced to think about liquidating one particular asset—an asset over which the powers of the world would trip to get their hands on . . . an asset that would allow the buyer to rule the world.

CHAPTER 4

The Devil's Deal

The bloody European events of 1914 ground away and spilled into 1915.

Wardenclyffe, Tesla's large, two-story, barn-like laboratory, was dwarfed by an imposing and surreal 200-foot-tall wooden structure, which was capped by a mushroom of electrodes and wires, looking like a tree version of Frankenstein.

Outside the building, against a cinderblock wall, Li was tending to a series of pigeon cages, carefully trading out the old newspapers in the bottom of each one with a fresh page. Li was engrossed in reading each page as he advanced from one cage to the next. The headline on the final page read:

PRESIDENT WILSON VOWS U.S. WILL REMAIN NEUTRAL ON EUROPE'S WAR!

Li muttered as he read the story . . .

"'Internationally untested United States, responding to inquiries by Britain's half-American Lord of the Admiralty, Mr. Winston Churchill . . .'"

Li looked up, said, "Hmm. Churchill is half American? Who knew?"

He continued reading. "' . . . declared neutrality'"

A pigeon dropping suddenly fell square on Wilson's photo's nose.

As Li shook the dropping off the sheet of newspaper, he saw a black, spanking new Cadillac Phaeton Tourer approaching down the road.

Li stuffed the pages in the cage, closed it, and ran inside.

In the lab, Tesla was standing with his eyes closed, serenely gripping a pulsing electrode in each hand, his hair standing on end, with a blue-white halo of electricity wafting around him.

Li burst in.

"Boss, Boss! I think they're here. The general and his secretary. Coming now."

Tesla lazily opened one eye and replied, "I believe you're referring to Lindley Miller Garrison, our secretary of war—doesn't see eye to eye with President Wilson, I understand. And the other fellow—probably not a general, Li. Maybe a major or a colonel. US Army Intelligence, at any rate. Show them in when they arrive, if you will, please."

"Right, Boss."

Li rushed back out. Tesla resumed his serene pose with the electrodes, his hair floating with static.

Two minutes later, Li padded back in with the two visitors in tow.

Secretary Garrison, tall, his hair parted down the middle, wearing a three-piece vested suit and rimless glasses, watched with intrigue as Li powered down the generator, Tesla's hair floated back into place, and he slowly opened his eyes.

"Gentlemen," he stated. "Welcome. Pardon my meditation exercise. It calms the body and fires the mind."

Garrison extended a cautious hand. Tesla declined it, nodding at the slowly unwinding generator.

"Still a live wire, Mr. Secretary. Wouldn't want to shock you, sir."

Garrison nodded and smiled.

Tesla looked at the man standing next to Garrison, glanced at his nametag and insignia.

"Major Smith. Glad to make your acquaintance."

Major Smith nodded, motioned toward Li, and asked, "Who's the Chinaman?"

"The 'Chinaman' is named Li. Li Yín Huŏ. He's my assistant."

"Can he be trusted?"

"You work US Army Intelligence, Major. Is that correct?"

Smith nodded. "That's correct."

"I've heard that army intelligence is an oxymoron. Can *you* be trusted, Major?"

Smith, unsure if he had just been insulted, looked at Garrison.

Garrison said, "How did Li end up in your custody, Mr. Tesla?"

"My dear friend Mark Twain won him in a card game. I won him from Twain in a game of rotation in a pool hall in San Francisco. Twain claims he let me win—told me I needed a minder. Why do you ask?"

"I have much respect for the late Mr. Twain," Garrison said. He looked at Smith and added, "As long as Mr. Li is trustworthy, I'm fine with him."

"Twain was never late," Li snapped.

"He's still not," Tesla added.

Smith looked at Li, said, "*Trustworthy*? He's barely civilized—how can he be trusted?"

"Oh, he's civilized, I assure you, Major," Tesla said. "He's a master of Kung Fu and the Five Animals of Shaolin. He speaks seven languages—I speak eight myself—and he's highly versed in Eastern philosophy." He paused and added, "As well as Western hypocrisy. How may *we* help you, gentlemen?"

Smith's jaw clenched at Tesla's insouciance.

Garrison said, "Mr. Tesla, do you have any knowledge of U-boats?"

"*Unterseeboots*?" Tesla replied with an intrigued look. "Ingenious contraptions. I happen to presently be working on alternative underwater communications and remote detection systems."

"Mr. Tesla," Garrison continued, "President Wilson has every intention of keeping us out of Europe's war."

"Despite the president's beliefs," Smith said, "Members of the military and I feel we have a moral obligation to help our British compatriots in their greatest hour of need. If Wilson doesn't have the balls to enter the war, by God, the least we can do is supply them with the means to defend themselves. Don't you agree, Mr. Tesla?"

"I believe the United States should do what it can, yes," Tesla replied. "What instructions did President Wilson give you prior to this visit?"

Garrison and Smith looked down at the floor.

"Ahh. I take it you are here without the approval—and therefore sans the knowledge of—the White House. Am I correct, gentlemen?"

"You are," Garrison said sheepishly. "But, Mr. Tesla . . . we need you, sir."

"Are you asking me to conspire to commit treason?"

"Treason? Of course not."

"Look," Smith piped in, "we only want you to help us build a submarine killing machine. Or something like that."

A sudden silence fell on the room.

Tesla looked from Garrison to Smith and back to Garrison.

"Do you gentlemen know anything about what I stand for? I'm not a warmonger. I'm a man of peace. Why, I'm practically a vegetarian. Apart from the odd steak and a stiff whiskey now and then."

"Mr. Tesla, nobody can do this but you. If it is anonymity you prefer, we'll report that someone else built the thing."

"Yes. Like that Italian guy, what's his name, Moroni?"

"Marconi, I believe you mean," Tesla said. "The man who stole a dozen of my patents to come up with my invention, the radio. If such a machine could be constructed, it could also be used to destroy lives."

"Or to save them," Garrison responded. "Countless numbers of innocent lives could be saved by preventing the damn Germans from continuing their reign of terror across Europe. It could help end this war before it goes on too much longer."

Li addressed Smith. "I understand you are arming merchant marine ships, Major Smith. Even some passenger liners are said to be bearing 4.7 inch guns. Is this correct?"

Garrison answered. "Winston Churchill, Britain's First Lord of the Admiralty, has given that order, yes. To protect the passengers."

"So, what's your point, Chinaman?" Smith growled at Li.

"After a torpedo is launched," Li said, "no matter how big the gun, if you can't see the sub approaching the boat from under the water—BOOM!—you're sunk. Even if the torpedo misses, you still see nothing to shoot back at. And if you see the sub, it's too late—you have no time to swivel the gun and fire before the sub lets loose its torpedo. You understand this?"

Smith looked at Li like he was speaking Chinese.

Tesla jumped in. "I believe what Li is saying is that first you have to locate the submarine. That, we may be able to help you with. We've been experimenting with bouncing and retrieving sonic vibrations that might prove useful if applied to this problem. It is worth discussing."

Smith stepped up to Tesla, looked him hard in the eyes, said, "Might prove useful? Like destroying a three-story steel building in New York?"

Tesla was taken off guard. He started to speak. Smith wasn't done.

"Oh yeah. We know what you're up to, Tesla," Smith continued. He waved an arm, indicating the spacious lab, and added, "We also know your ungodly Wardenclyffe pipe dream here is deep in the red. Morgan isn't going to give you another dime—and you know it. I'm well aware of the luxurious lifestyle you enjoy. The company you keep. The bills you rack up living at the Waldorf-Astoria. Room 1748 to be exact."

Tesla looked down at the intelligence officer for a long moment, then stated firmly, "Gentlemen, you may go now."

He walked to the door and opened it. Li bowed respectfully at Garrison and Smith, waved a hand toward the door, and gave them an inscrutable smile.

After a brief stare-down, they exited.

Outside, Garrison's driver opened the door of the big Cadillac, and Garrison and Smith got in. Tesla and Li watched as the car drove away. They walked back inside Wardenclyffe.

Inside, Li closed and bolted the heavy door. Tesla treaded to a large object, mostly hidden by a canvas tarp. He threw the tarp back, revealing a cross between a turn-of-the-century cannon and a futuristic ray gun: the same oscillator pulse weapon that would be recovered from the *Lusitania* thirty-four years in the future.

"What are you thinking, Boss?" Li asked.

Tesla said nothing as he examined the partially completed contraption.

At length, he said, "Li . . . maybe we should consider turning a failed experiment into much needed capital. I wonder what Twain would advise."

"From where I stand," a voice announced from behind them, "it looks like the devil's deal, my friend."

Tesla's serious countenance melted into a grin before he even turned to address Mark Twain, who stood there, white suit gleaming, stroking his superb moustache.

"Twain!" Tesla cried out joyfully, padding quickly toward Twain. "What took you so long, my friend!?"

"I've been traveling, Nicky. Traveling the universe. You were right—it's magnificent!"

Li looked at Tesla like he was off his rocker. His eyes went from Tesla's face to the empty spot Tesla was addressing and back to Tesla.

Li asked nervously, "B-boss? Y-you okay?"

Tesla and Twain embraced, clapping each other on the back.

"Look, Twain, here's my thinking—correct me if I'm seeing it wrong here," Tesla began, excitedly filling Twain in. "It shoots sound waves, not bullets. It's a self-*defensive* device—not an offensive weapon. It's really as simple as that."

"Ah," Twain responded, "therein lies the trap: when a man makes a decision based solely on financial needs, he is prone to make grave miscalculations. Remember, all wars are started on the basis of land and resources—someone wants real estate or natural resources the other guy has, and that someone doesn't want to pay for them. Then the politicians slap a less gauche excuse onto the plan—usually having to do with religious disagreements or simple crude patriotic fervor—and voilà: war. And so what is the essence of war?"

"Greed," Tesla replied dolefully.

"Precisely. War is greed—the language of the devil. So, for you, that brings up one important question: do you really *need* Wardenclyffe? After all, Nicky, was it not created in the first place by *mere thought*?"

"By God, Twain, you're right! *Thought creates!* If I could create all this from ideas in my mind, if I brought it to life from thought to reality, then—"

"You can do it again—without accepting the devil's deal."

"True . . . but what if I approach it simply as the means of completing an invention my mind conjured up in the first place?"

"Let's explore that," Twain replied.

By now, Li—who was looking at Tesla, whose arm was held straight out in front of him while chatting to no one—was thinking the great Nikola Tesla had finally slid off his rocker.

"B-boss?" he asked timidly. "You okay? Who're you talking to?"

Twain and Tesla suddenly stopped talking, turned in unison, and faced Li.

"You know, dear Nicky," Twain said, tugging at one end of his moustache, "you are eventually going to have to explain to Mr. Li how to see me *physically*. Otherwise, you'll drive him nuts."

"I already do drive him nuts, dear Twain. I already do."

CHAPTER 5

America Joins the War

As they drove away from Wardenclyffe, Secretary Garrison jotted notes in a leather binder while Smith sullenly stared out the window from the seat next to him.

"We let him off too easily," Smith sulked.

Garrison smacked his pen down on the pad, turned sharply, and said, "A *sub killing machine*!? Have you not done your homework, Major? Do you not know Tesla's social proclivities?! A man like him must be lured, led, *convinced* to go against his principles. You don't come at a high intellect like his with a hammer in the face! If you do, you'll find you have lost all initiative, and most likely he will cleverly destroy your career by making you look like a fool!"

"Like to see him try."

"Force is not the point!" Garrison took a breath. Composed himself. Stated more calmly, "I would have liked to have eased into it with a little more grace, Major. You get my point?"

"You've never experienced the whistle and thud of an artillery shell coming in on you, have you, Mr. Secretary?" He continued before Garrison could reply, "You're a lawyer, a *politician*," he spat derisively. "One doesn't *ease into* war."

"We are not waging war on Mr. Tesla, Major, we're trying to—"

"An artillery shell gives you about two seconds of 'grace' as you call it," Smith cut him off. "Then, *boom!*"

"I do not pretend to understand your firsthand accounts of combat, Major."

"Then let me paint the picture for you: you look the survivors in the eyes and you know what to expect from them when the next one whistles overhead. I was firing a warning shot across Tesla's bow, Mr. Secretary. *That's* war."

"And tell me, Major: what did Tesla's eyes tell you?"

"They told me that no matter how many shells we drop on him, he will not be influenced by fear and intimidation."

"You're the one who wanted to choose that route, not me. And now I'm left to mop up after you. I'd be surprised if he allows us in Wardenclyffe again."

"There'll be no need for that. I saw something else in his eyes, Mr. Secretary: Tesla is a dreamer."

"And that helps us how?"

"We offer him a bigger dream."

* * *

As August 1914 gave way to September, the Allies retreated to the River Marne. On August 25, Japan declared war on Austria-Hungary. The following day, British and French forces conquered Togoland, a German protectorate in West Africa, while the Allies retreated from the Battle of Le Cateau. Through the last week of August and into the first week of November, British and Japanese forces captured the German-controlled port of Tsingtao in China, the Royal Navy won the First Battle of Heligoland Bight in the North Sea, the Allies retreated in the Battle of Saint Quentin, and the Austro-Hungarians were defeated in the Battle of Rava Russka.

During the second week of September, at the First Battle of the Marne, the German advance on Paris was stopped, but the Russian Army of the Neman was forced from East Prussia with heavy casualties. Then, on September 22, the German light cruiser SMS *Emden* attacked Madras, Spain, and the following week, the Germans attacked and captured Antwerp, Belgium.

On October 5, 1914, young British military officer Winston Churchill was sent to Antwerp to assist Belgian government forces, along with the Royal Marine Brigade and the 1st and 2nd Naval Brigades, in evacuating the city. Antwerp fell on October 10, taking 2,500 military casualties.

The war had only just begun. And casualties were piling up in sickening numbers on both sides, with no clear victor in sight.

Drastic measures had to be taken.

In London, in the war room of the British Parliament, an auspicious group of men had gathered to try to resolve the deepening gloom and mayhem the world was undergoing.

Seated near the great table in a cloud of cigar smoke was Prime Minister Herbert Henry Asquith, 1st Earl of Oxford and Asquith. An ideal peacetime manager, Asquith was seen as being out of his depth as the Great War increased its grip across the continent. The unsure and often vacillating prime minister had struggled to put across the image of a dynamic, decisive leader, and the British public was becoming increasingly uncertain of victory.

Seated next to the prime minister was War Secretary Horatio Herbert Kitchener, highly experienced and deeply respected among his military peers. Kitchener, sporting a thick and dramatic moustache, was draped in so many medals they looked like a coat of gold armor across his broad chest.

Seated across from Prime Minister Asquith and War Secretary Kitchener, was Admiral of the Fleet John Arbuthnot "Jacky" Fisher. Famous for initiating naval reforms that had helped make Britain the dominant power on the oceans of the world, Fisher began his naval career in wooden sailing ships armed with muzzle-loading cannon. He continued his career in the navy all the way to steel-hulled battle cruisers, submarines, and even up until the first aircraft carriers. Argumentative, energetic, and progressive, Fisher's renown in the British Navy was bested only by that of Lord Nelson.

Seated next to Admiral Jackie Fisher was First Lord of the Admiralty Winston Churchill. A member of the British aristocracy, of the Dukes of Marlborough, a branch of the Spencer family, Churchill was the son of Lord Randolph Churchill, who had served as chancellor of the Exchequer, and Jennie Jerome Churchill, an American socialite.

No stranger to war, as a young army officer, Churchill had seen action in British India, the Sudan, the Second Boer War, and now, the Great War.

The men hovered over a massive oak table upon which was sprawled a map spanning the British Isles to Western Russia. Small wooden ships, tanks, and battalions of soldiers, representing the different forces engaged in the battle, were carefully arranged across the map, placed in their known positions.

With a long, wooden pointer, Churchill tapped the sea blockade of the English Channel and then pointed to the lands covering most of Europe.

"Gentlemen," Churchill drawled, "this territory here now belongs to the enemy, Germany. Our blockade is starving the Kaiser, Germany, and Austria-Hungary. We own the seven seas. Inward and outward sailings are suffering minimal losses."

"Tell that to the German U-boat captains," Asquith stated.

Fisher stood and began pacing. The medals on his uniform jangled like jailer's keys as he treaded back and forth. "Yet your 'minimal losses' at sea continue to rise," Fisher snapped. "The only thing keeping the arms flowing from America is the protection of Her Majesty's Naval escorts." He looked at the map and added, "And the passenger liners."

"The Germans would never sink a liner carrying American passengers," Kitchener said. "They'd risk war with the Americans. The liners are safe."

"Without the strength of the United States, however," Asquith said, rubbing his chin as he examined the map, "I am not at all confident that we will prevail, gentlemen."

A smile crept across the cherubic face of Winston Churchill as he used his pointer to push a neutral ship into the map's war zone.

He removed his cigar from his mouth and stated, "Why don't we invite the Yankees to the party and find out?"

Churchill knocked the ship over on its side.

"What the devil do you mean, Churchill?" Asquith asked, annoyed.

Kitchener and Fisher looked at Churchill, looked at each other, and nodded.

Meanwhile, at the same moment, inside the German High Command war room, a circular room with deep red walls containing framed portraits of military conquests, Kaiser Wilhelm II was standing at the head of an oval table, across from Grand Admiral Alfred Peter Friedrich von Tirpitz with his distinctive split, two-tailed beard. Tirpitz, as secretary of state of the German Imperial Naval Office, was famous for having built up the Imperial Navy into a world-class machine to be reckoned with—one that could give a good run to the dominant British Royal Navy. The German Imperial Navy, while the second largest in the world, was only 60 percent of the size and power of the vaunted British Royal Navy. To make up the difference, Tirpitz had turned to submarine warfare. The German Navy could now strike fear into the British. In fact, the one big sea battle the two had engaged in, the Battle of Jutland, ended with both sides claiming victory. Tirpitz's expansion of his navy greatly alarmed the Brits and jump-started an expensive arms race, pushing the British into a mutual aid agreement with the French.

Standing next to Grand Admiral Tirpitz was Vizeadmiral, Chief of the Admiralty Staff, and Commander of the German

High Seas Fleet Hugo von Pohl. Admiral Pohl, a cautious and calculating man, was leery of taking on the British Grand Fleet. His weapon of choice on the high seas was unrestricted submarine warfare, a policy he initiated on the very first day he took over the German fleet in early 1915.

However, the Declaration of Paris had formalized the rules for naval engagements involving civilian vessels. The so-called Cruiser Rules required that the crew and passengers of civilian ships be safeguarded before a ship could be confiscated or sunk. The rules required that merchant ships fly their own flag and not pretend to be of a different nationality. The target ship was required to stop when confronted by an enemy vessel, allow itself to be boarded and searched, and was not allowed to be armed or to take hostile or evasive actions.

"I want more kills!" Wilhelm said, slamming his palms on the table. "Weapons and munitions continue to reach the British forces!"

"Rules of conduct are hindering our success and putting our *unterseeboot* fleet at great risk, mein Kaiser," Pohl spat derisively. "This, this, Declaration of Paris, has hurt us. Cruiser Rules!? Bah! Surface and give warning. Insanity! It is the nature of our submarines to strike and then to disappear. It is not our concern that commercial vessels are attempting to enter and depart British waters, trying to help replenish England's dwindling resources. Our waiting around and asking permission to do what needs to be done is only prolonging Germany's glorious victory, mein herr!"

Tirpitz nodded in agreement.

"Herr Kaiser, we need unrestricted submarine authorization. How can a U-boat glide beneath the seas, spot a target, then surface, announce our presence, and ask the passengers to disembark while we sink their vessel? We may as well scrap our U-boat fleet altogether!"

"Yes, mein herr," Pohl piped in. "We did not agree to this Cruiser Rule. It must be broken—or our navy will be broken by the British fleet. The only area we can outgun them on the high seas is beneath the seas."

"Very well," Wilhelm announced, "you may have your unrestricted submarine warfare in the waters around Britain. Henceforth, any neutral ships, including those of the United States should she be foolishly inclined to join the effort on behalf of her British cousins, will be attacked. *Without* warning."

The admirals smiled.

Britain was doomed.

CHAPTER 6

The Oscillator Pulse Weapon Test

Late one afternoon on a large, flat barge, tethered to an old concrete dock offshore on the Thames River in Connecticut, Tesla lowered his binoculars from a point he had been examining out on the water. Fifty feet behind him, Li was working under camouflage netting that was concealing Tesla's oscillator pulse weapon. On the dock, a dozen armed soldiers stood guard.

Tesla brought the binoculars back up to his eyes as Major Smith approached him.

"What's the periscope I just saw in the river?" Tesla asked without looking at Smith.

"One of the first submarines Holland made," Smith replied. "An iron coffin. Built for the bottom and for staying there, we used to say. Navy plans to use it for our UBT program. Underwater Bomb Testing. Blow it to smithereens."

Tesla said nothing. He lowered the glasses. He treaded back toward the oscillator pulse weapon. Smith fell in behind him. Smith checked his watch.

Li was scrutinizing Smith. Smith made eye contact with him, stopped, addressed him sharply.

"What are you looking at?"

Li looked at him but said nothing.

Tesla turned and faced Smith.

"Must be nice to have a slave," Smith said to Tesla.

"He's my *assistant*," Tesla corrected him calmly.

"I prefer my assistants to wear skirts."

"Then perhaps you need to hire Scotsmen."

Smith drilled Tesla a look. Then he chuckled, shook his finger at him, and said, "A genius *and* a comedian. I like that combination in a slave owner."

"And how does your owner, the US government, feel about you?"

Before Smith could respond, Garrison's Cadillac rounded the corner of a derelict structure on the dock and stopped next to the barge's mooring line.

Garrison got out, walked down gangway, and joined Tesla, Li, and Smith on the deck.

"Nikola, my friend," Garrison smiled, grabbed Tesla's hand, and gave it a shake. "How are you?"

He stepped past Tesla and headed toward the gun.

Tesla pulled a handkerchief from his pocket and wiped his hand.

"May I take a look at it?" Garrison asked as he reached the device.

A loud, shrieking whistle suddenly pierced the air. All heads turned to see Smith taking a whistle from his mouth and waving a hand at the soldiers. The soldiers climbed into a truck and drove out of sight.

Smith faced Garrison and said, "Just a precaution, Secretary Garrison."

Garrison looked at Tesla and asked, "Are we in harm's way here, Mr. Tesla?"

"I'm strictly talking about security, sir," Smith said to Garrison. "If it succeeds, the fewer eyes on this thing, the better. Even less if it fails."

Garrison looked inquiringly at Tesla.

"You needn't worry, gentlemen," Tesla said. "As long as we remain away from the barrel, we'll be safe."

Tesla looked at Smith who was still holding his whistle.

"May we demonstrate for Secretary Garrison, or would you like another toot on your little whistle?"

Smith looked at him for a beat, unsure whether to respond or blow the thing just to irritate the scientist. He scanned the perimeter: no one in sight but the four of them on the barge. He nodded his assent.

Li pulled back the tarp, revealing the oscillator pulse weapon, bolted to the metal deck. It was the same gun from Tesla's lab, though now modified with eight harmonic oscillators surrounding the barrel, making it look like a big ray gun mounted on a tripod.

Tesla picked up a wooden case that had wires running to the gun.

Li lowered a cone-shaped metal dish into the water directly in line with the gun and the submarine.

"What can we expect, Mr. Tesla?" Garrison asked.

"Li is securing our receiver and—despite Major Smith's fear—the only excitement is going to be on this meter in my hands."

"I never said I was afraid," barked Smith.

Tesla opened the case, revealing a glass-faced meter with a needle pointing toward its bottom, which was marked off with distance gradations leading up to a red bar at the top.

Tesla tapped the meter and said, "If successful, we will not only locate your submarine, Mr. Secretary, but also we'll be able to determine within an allowance of ten feet how far away it is from us and whether it is advancing toward us or retreating from us."

"That iron coffin is up to its conning tower in silt," Smith said. "Not much chance it'll be coming at us."

"If you'll give us just a moment, gentlemen, Li and I will—as I believe your type puts it, Major Smith—lock and load."

"*My type*? Just shoot the damn thing, Tesla."

"Not to disappoint you, Major Smith, but it doesn't 'shoot' in the sense you're thinking. However, this is the dangerous part, so I would recommend you retreat a few steps to be on the safe side."

"You told us as long as we're not on the business end of the gun, we're okay."

Tesla tapped his chest, which produced a dull metallic sound, as if he was wearing a protective plate under his clothing.

"Special protection. Just a precaution, really," Tesla responded.

Smith looked at him. Then he reluctantly stepped back and stood next to Garrison.

Tesla walked over to Li at the gun.

He whispered to Tesla, "What special protection, Boss?"

Tesla indicated Smith, smiled, and tapped his chest again, eliciting the same dull metallic thud. Tesla turned to shield himself from Smith and Garrison's look and showed Li that it was only a pocket watch, hanging by a cord around his neck.

"Subterfuge, Li. Don't want to let them think they know everything that's happening."

Tesla flipped open the watch cover. Li pulled a pair of aviator goggles out of a bag and put them on. Tesla noticed that the second hand on his watch was running backward. He shook it, held it to his ear, and looked at it again.

Tesla said to Li, "Remind me to add a timepiece to their bill."

He looked at Li in the biplane goggles and said, "Li, I told you, you don't need those."

"I want them," Li grinned. "Makes me feel like a space man."

Li opened the heavy lid near the rear of the gun and turned a wheel, unlocking the top. Tesla opened a padded case.

Inside was the power core, wrapped in a Waldorf linen napkin. It had a similar appearance to the cylindrical device that had destroyed itself in the electrical storm in front of Tesla's lab months earlier in New York. Li carefully transferred the core to Tesla. Its industrial grade bronze ends were capped in a heavy glass tube. Inside, the contraption was glowing blue-white with charged particles, like lightning in a bottle.

Tesla lowered the core, fitting it perfectly into place. Li secured the top, locking it into the breech of the gun.

A humming sound began to build. Li trained the binoculars on the river.

Tesla treaded back to joined Garrison and Smith.

"Is it ready to go, Mr. Tesla?" Garrison asked.

Tesla looked at Li and said, "Li, it's in your hands now. Fire when ready."

"I would have thought you would want to man the thing," Smith said, adding with a chuckle, "Are you afraid?"

"Not at all," Tesla replied. "I'm into results." He held up the box with the gauge in it. "Curse of the scientist. I want to see the instruments at work. Besides, it keeps the little boy in Li alive."

Li was gripping the oscillator pulse weapon as if he were Buck Rogers himself.

The humming intensified, echoing off the surrounding structures.

Garrison and Smith looked from the gaugc to the water and back again. Nothing was happening. The needle on the gauge vibrated a bit, but it wasn't moving upward.

"Doesn't appear to be working, Mr. Tesla," Smith said. "Assuming that red mark on the gauge there is Bingo."

"Patience, Major. It seems to be performing perfectly from where I'm sitting. We are looking beyond our target, down the river, and out to sea. Science is comparatives, Major Smith. Li, take it to 70 percent and proceed to primary target."

Li turned a brass wheel and the oscillator pulse weapon rotated toward the periscope and submarine below it. The humming grew to the sound of howling thunder.

Garrison raised the binoculars to his eyes, trained it on the periscope, and adjusted the focus.

"I don't see anything happening at all," he called out, dialing to refocus again.

Major Smith shook his head, looked at the ground, and muttered something under his breath having to do with crackpots and mad scientists.

“That thing can’t even find a sixty ton sitting duck!” he shouted over the humming and began laughing.

Li suddenly shouted, “Three . . . Two . . . One!”

Tesla yelled, “It’s happening right here, right now, gentlemen. Look.”

They all looked at the gauge. The needle was shooting deep into the red and registering the distance to the target.

Tesla said, “Three hundred thirty-three meters. One thousand feet.” He looked at Smith and added, “And that, my friend, is Bingo!”

“Son of a bitch and halleluiah!” Smith shouted joyfully as he peered out at the calm water.

“Good work, Mr. Tesla,” Garrison said. “Very good work. This should please President Wilson and the Allied forces.”

Garrison raised his binoculars in the direction of the distant submarine.

“Gotcha,” he quipped.

From behind them came a rattling metallic sound. Tesla looked back . . . and saw the hubcap from the Cadillac Phaeton Tourer lazily roll off the dock and *ker-plunk* right into the water.

The four men turned in unison to look at the secretary’s Caddy. The car was shuddering violently. Lug nuts were unscrewing, running boards sprang off, the hood and trunk door vibrated violently open.

The loud humming sound was gradually eclipsed by a screeching sound like a thousand fingernails on a thousand chalkboards.

The men clapped their hands over their ears. Garrison’s binoculars suddenly started to come apart in his hands. He flung them to the ground.

"What's happening!?" he shouted.

The looks on their faces changed to sheer horror.

"What the hell!?" Smith cried out.

The vibrating increased. The men began to shake from the shuddering.

Tesla looked down at the metal barge beneath his feet. Large bolts holding the barge together were shaking free.

Garrison's Cadillac was shuddering itself to pieces.

"Li!" Tesla shouted. "Turn it off! TURN IT OFF!"

But it was too late. The end of the barrel was glowing red. A lightning bolt arced out, shot across the water, and struck the periscope dead on. A strange eruption bubbled from below and then—KA-*BOOM*!—a huge geyser exploded into a cloud of water and debris. Iron plating and rivets filled the air like shrapnel.

Tesla, Garrison, and Smith ran for cover.

Li, grinning like a lunatic at the havoc whirling around them, cried out, "Oh yes, yes, Boss!" and shut the device down.

The lightning bolt vanished. Everything went deathly quiet. Smith peeked out from behind a metal railing. Garrison peered at his Cadillac. It had stopped shaking. The hood and trunk slammed shut.

Everyone let out a nervous breath. Slowly they stood. Uneasy. Cautious. Hearts jackhammering. And then—the sound of an incoming whistle came from above them. They all looked up and saw the submarine's conning tower whizzing down at them from the sky like a missile . . . and landing dead center on Garrison's luxury Cadillac Phaeton Tourer.

Garrison's jaw dropped.

Smith's eyes darted everywhere, assessing what had just happened.

Li was grinning like a cat with two rats.

Tesla muttered confidently, "Hmmm. Seems to be a minor miscalculation somewhere. Not to worry. I'll work it out."

Smith looked from the speared Cadillac to the churning water to Dr. Nikola Tesla.

"Tesla," he shouted exultantly, "you're a freaking damn genius! It worked! Like a bat out of hell, the thing worked!"

Garrison shouted, "What do you mean it worked, you moron! Look what it did to my Caddy!"

"Caddy hell—it destroyed the submarine!" Smith shot back. "A whole damn submarine! Sixty tons of river pig iron, up in smoke, like paper in the wind!"

Garrison looked around them. The import of what just happened dawned on him finally.

He nodded slowly. "By God, Major, you're right. It did work! Just like we hoped it would—twice as good, in fact!"

Garrison jabbed a finger at Smith and ordered, "Major, double the guard. Cover it and secure it. I want this thing moved to the Navy Yard in New London."

"Hold on, Mr. Secretary," Tesla said. "That was not our agreement. This is my property and I alone decide its fate. What you witnessed today was not some grand success. Rather, it was a failure that could have resulted in great bodily harm—even death, to any of us here. It needs recalibrating, fine-tuning, and rebuilding."

Li called out from the gun, "The breech is fused, Boss. It's melted shut."

Garrison and Smith looked at each other for a beat.

"All right, Dr. Tesla," Garrison said, "Maybe you're right. It would be useless without you. And Li. I'll tell you what: it will be shipped back to Wardenclyffe as agreed. But Mr. Tesla, be advised that what we witnessed today will be subject to further discussion with the White House. Understood?"

"I say we appropriate it now," Smith snapped.

"I'm in charge here, Major," Garrison shot back. "Now stand down."

Smith looked away, his jaw clenching.

Garrison looked at Tesla. Tesla shrugged noncommittally.

Garrison stared at him a moment longer and then said, "Very well. It is agreed. Good day, Doctor. A very good day, indeed."

Smith shot a look at Tesla as if he wanted to say something, but he turned and trudged off in the direction the military vehicle had gone earlier.

"I'd offer you a ride," Garrison said, looking at his Cadillac, "but it seems I will be the guest of Major Smith's men for transportation."

"Li and I have made arrangements for lodging in town," Tesla replied. "I would just as soon stay with the pulse weapon, anyway, to see it safely back home."

Tesla nodded in the direction of Smith, treading down the road. "You'd better not miss your ride, Mr. Secretary. It's a long walk if you do."

Garrison nodded. "Right. We'll be in touch soon."

He turned and walked briskly away, catching up with Major Smith. As the two ambled down the road together, Tesla could hear them talking in low, excited tones, like two men who had just won the lottery.

And in a way, they had.

"Be careful what you wish for, gentlemen," Tesla said under his breath as he watched them disappear around a bend.

CHAPTER 7

CLAIRE

That night, Tesla and Li arrived in front of the Widow's Nest Hotel, an ancient New London, Connecticut establishment, not exactly in the same league as the Waldorf-Astoria.

They approached the front door. Tesla looked to the right and to the left, then commented, "No doorman. How decidedly *downtown*."

Li quipped, "Not everyone is used to the Waldorf like you are, Boss."

Tesla asked, "Are we checked in?"

"Yes, Boss. Checked in this morning while you were setting up at the river."

"Bags in the room?"

"Yep," Li replied. "And all unpacked, Boss. Just like you like."

"Excellent," Tesla said, gripping the door handle. "Shall we?"

Li nodded. Tesla pulled the door open. They stepped into the lobby.

The place was bustling. The patrons were middle to lower class, blue-collar workers, a few white-collar types. Not one person of color. Except a brown-skinned lad bussing tables in the bar across the lobby. And an older black fellow manning the elevator.

Tesla looked down at the worn, dark carpet. He sniffed the musty air. He made a face and shook his head.

"Quaint," he said. "Was there nothing else available in New London, Li?"

"Boss," Li grinned, "sometimes you're stuck up."

"Better than being stuck here."

A laughing man and woman were walking toward them. Spotting Tesla and Li, their laughter ceased. As they passed the pair, the woman smiled at Tesla. The man pulled the woman close to him, scowling at Li as they walked by.

"Now *that* is stuck up, my dear Li," Tesla said. "Why he looked down on you when they apparently live *here* is anyone's guess."

Tesla's eyes took in the surroundings, his mind scanning, analyzing, assessing.

"This is a different crowd," he announced. "Not exactly an enlightened bunch, I perceive, Li. Therefore, I suggest we make a pact not to be conspicuous this evening, no matter what. We keep a low profile. Agreed?"

Li crossed his heart, nodded, and said, "Like a Chinaman in San Francisco, Boss. Head down, mouth closed, play dumb."

Ahead of them, on the other side of the lobby, was the entrance to the bar.

"There. Let's try the bar," Tesla said, nodding in that direction. "I doubt if they have port or even a decent Cabernet Sauvignon, but they surely must have whiskey, by the looks of the place."

They padded across the worn carpet to the bar.

The bartender had been watching them since they'd entered the hotel lobby. As they stepped into the bar, his face registered disapproval.

"We won't be serving the likes of him around here," he said, nodding at Li while pretending to mop up the countertop with a rag.

"My good man," Tesla said importantly, "we are checked into this hotel and we plan on spending good money on the best meal your restaurant can provide. But first, I want to enjoy a fine cigar, a glass of your best whiskey, and a game or two of billiards. You do provide those amenities, don't you?"

The bartender stared at him. Tesla pulled an Indian head $5 gold coin from his waistcoat pocket, announced, "My assistant Li here will sit quietly in a corner. Out of sight. Out of mind. Bothering no one. Do we agree?"

He slapped the coin down on the bar. The bartender reached out, took it, and bit it, looking at Tesla suspiciously.

He nodded, pocketed the coin, and mumbled, "I guess we do." He jerked his head toward some chairs in the corner and said, "Sit anywhere you like. As long as it's over there."

As Tesla and Li turned to take a seat, the bartender grabbed Li by the collar and said, "And you behave yourself. Hear?"

Li instinctively stiffened when he felt the grip of the man's fist on his jacket. Tesla shot Li a look.

Li relaxed, plastered on a goofy grin, stuck out his front teeth, and said to the bartender in a caricature of a Chinaman accent,

"Oh, yes, you betchu, master. Behave velly, velly well. No pee on floor, nothing. I plomise you."

Tesla rolled his eyes.

The bartender let Li go, grumbling, "That's more like it."

As Tesla and Li walked to a table in the back corner, Tesla said under his breath to Li, "Sometimes I can't take you anywhere, Li."

Unwelcoming looks were thrown their way as they threaded through the tables.

They approached a table where an attractive young lady was trying to eat dinner while a rowdy group of sailors and bowery toughs stood pressed around her, beer mugs in hand, trying to engage her in conversation and impress her with their lack of couth.

"Come on, love, give us your name at least," one man drunkenly pestered her.

Prim and polite, she bravely ignored the group and continued eating, nodding now and then as they peppered questions at her.

"*Prissy*, I bet her name is," one lug guffawed. "She looks like a prissy li'l thing."

The others bellowed in laughter.

"If you must know," she answered politely, "my name is Claire. Now, I would be very grateful if you kind gentlemen would please leave me in peace while I finish my dinner."

"Kind gentlemen!" they roared in laughter.

As Tesla and Li worked their way past the group, Li's eyes momentarily glimpsed Claire through the crowd of ruffians. Tesla, fixated on a billiard game ahead of them, barely gave the woman a glance.

They stopped at the billiard table just as a guy who was as big as a moose smartly snapped the cue ball on an impressive winning shot.

"Well played," Tesla exclaimed. He leaned to Li and said excitedly, "Li, did you see what he just did—that fellow there, big as a moose? Double bank shot, sixty-three degrees, back-spinning to thirty-one degrees on the second bank at half speed, with just enough English to stop the cue ball cold—right on the lip. Brilliant."

The shooter grabbed his beer mug and downed a sloppy gulp as Tesla approached him.

"Bravo, my man!" Tesla told him. "What's your name?"

"Moose," he said, drilling Tesla with a look.

"How appropriate!" Tesla said delightedly.

"And I'm not *your man*," Moose continued, dragging a sleeve across his mouth.

"I didn't mean it in the perjorat—"

"I don't know what you said back there, Slick," Moose cut him off, "but why don't you put your money where your mouth is, and I'll be happy to take it away from you."

"Excellent idea!" Tesla grinned.

He shrugged out of his suit coat and handed it to Li.

Tesla smiled at Moose and said, "What do you say, Moose—ten bucks a ball?"

Moose looked at Tesla like he had a screw loose.

"What are you, some kind of pool shark dandy?" he scowled.

He tossed his cue stick on the table and treaded over to the group of men gathered around Claire.

Tesla, a look of confusion on his face as he watched Moose walk away, said to Li, "Was it something I said?"

"Never mind, Boss," Li said. "Like you said, this is a different crowd. Not exactly enlightened. I'm going to find us a table."

"Very well, I'm going to thrash one of these hapless hooligans in a game of billiards if it's the last thing I do tonight. It's all about math, trajectory, inertia, and angles, you know."

"I know, Boss. You told me that before. I'll go find us a table."

Li threaded his way to a table in the corner, conveniently with a direct view of Claire. He sat down with his back against the wall and tried not to stare at Claire, across the room. He failed miserably.

Li watched as a man as wide as a small house leaned to Claire and said drunkenly, "No need you eatin' all alone when you got me right here, little lady."

Moose suggestively added, "Yeah. We'll be your friends for the night."

Claire fiddled absentmindedly with the lace on her collar and said firmly, "Gentlemen, if I want your friendship, I will let you know. In the meantime, *please*, allow me finish my dinner in peace."

Moose and House roared with laughter, sloshing beer onto Claire's table. She let out a small shriek when she didn't quite make it out of the way of the spilling suds.

Li rose smoothly from his chair.

Meanwhile, at the billiard table, as Tesla lined up his shot at the cue ball, his eyes caught sight of Li slowly slinking like a cat on prey.

Tesla's head swiveled to follow Li's trajectory. His eyes lined up on the rowdies converged around the table with the pretty woman, now dabbing beer off her lace blouse.

"Oh God, Li," Tesla muttered to himself. "Not again, not now—not *here*."

"Playing alone, Tesla?" came a familiar voice behind Tesla.

He withdrew from the shot and turned around to see Major Smith, chalking up a pool cue.

"I am not surprised to see you here, Major," Tesla said tersely, trying to keep one eye on the creeping Li and one on Smith.

"Of course you would see me here. You didn't think Secretary Garrison was just going to leave you to your own devices with the pulse weapon, did you?"

"No, I meant I'm not surprised to see you, because this is just your type of place, Major. Now, how can I help you?"

"You've got something we want, Tesla. I'm here to see that no harm comes to it."

Smith saw that Tesla's attention was elsewhere. He turned in the direction Tesla was looking and saw Li padding stealthily toward the men surrounding Claire.

Smith turned back to Tesla and added, "Or your yellow dog there."

House and Moose had no clue Li had come up behind them. Moose was trying to dab beer off Claire's blouse against her protests.

"Excuse me, fine gentleman," Li said politely to Moose and House.

Moose and House turned abruptly and looked at Li standing there.

"What do you want, boy?!" Moose sneered.

Li's hand flicked out and swiped Moose's hand from Claire's blouse.

"Please allow this lovely young lady her meal in peace," Li said sternly. "She has made it clear that your attention is unwelcome."

Moose and House rose up drunkenly to their full heights—which were considerably taller and wider than Li's.

Li smiled up at them.

"Who are you to say what she likes, chink!?" House bellowed.

"Little yellow bastard shouldn't even be in here!" Moose roared. "Barkeep!" he yelled at the bartender across the room, "I thought this was an Americans only establishment!"

Moose suddenly swung a ham-sized fist at Li.

Li deftly ducked the swing, did a small jump, and snapped a hook kick, landing a foot to the side of Moose's head.

Moose groaned as he was slammed back and smashed into a table.

Beer mugs flew. Beer flew. Fists flew.

House lunged, throwing a fist at Li's face. Li grabbed the fist in mid-swing, gave it a slight wrench. The bone snapped. Li deftly stepped aside and, using House's continuing forward momentum, pulled him by the wrist straight into the wall.

Smith watched from across the room, impressed with Li's moves, but not making a move to help him.

Tesla said calmly to Smith, "Oh, don't worry about helping him, Major Smith—not that you were planning to. Li is quite capable of defending himself."

Tesla turned back to the action just as a pool stick smashed into Li's head. Li caught himself from falling, turned—a moment too late, as Moose's fist crashed into his mouth, sending him staggering toward the pool table. More goons rushed at Li, shoving him into the pool table and knocking Smith aside in the process.

Smith brushed himself off, handed his cue stick to Tesla and said, "Looks like he can use a hand now. Time to join the party!"

Smith grabbed a pool ball in each hand, waded into the mêlée, smashing balls into heads and stomachs, knocking drunks left and right, which allowed Li to leap up and face the swinging thugs.

Li gave Smith a short nod of thanks. He and Smith took on three more attackers.

Tesla threw a pool stick to Li, shouting, "Behind you!"

Li caught the stick midair and became a blur of swinging stick and flying feet. Bones cracked. Groans of pain followed bodies as they thudded to the floor.

Tesla took a sip of whiskey from his highball glass and grinned as he watched the unlikely contradiction of Li and Smith shoulder to shoulder handily taking on a bar full of drunken louts.

Soon, House and Moose were lying in a bloody heap, moaning in pain. Others were passed out cold. Still others were stumbling or crawling toward the exit.

Heaving for breath, Smith watched with envy as Li, fresh as a daisy, crashed the pool cue across the face of the last man standing. Li dragged a sleeve across his bloody mouth, tossed the stick to the floor, turned to Smith, smiled, brushed off his hands, and held one out to Smith.

Smith glared at Li. Looked down at his outstretched hand. Slapped it away and raised his bloodied fists.

"This isn't over, Li," he said. "Not as long as a Chinaman is standing, it ain't."

Li looked confused, as if he wasn't sure Smith was serious.

"Come on, chink," Smith barked. "Do you want a shot at the title? Right here and now. Unless you're afraid."

Li's hand slowly lowered. He looked at Smith. Shook his head sadly. He turned and treaded toward the exit.

Suddenly, Moose sprang up, pulled a knife from his boot, and charged at Li.

"Li!" Claire cried out. "*Dàotuì*!"

Li was so surprised to hear a warning shouted at him in Mandarin from Claire's lips that he abruptly stopped and turned to look at her just as Moose yelled, "Chink bastard, I'll slice you from throat to gut!" and swung—his blade cutting through Li's coat and slashing his right shoulder.

Li fell back, off balance, and tried to face Moose as the big man charged at him again. As Moose raised the knife to finish Li off, he was suddenly smashed across the jaw by a pool stick, wielded by Major Smith.

Moose went down like an overfed baby at naptime.

Smith threw what was left of the pool cue to the floor, muttered at Li, "This ain't over, yellow man," and strode to the bar, wiping blood from his face.

As Li watched Smith order a whiskey, he shook his head and said under his breath, "That is one confused soldier."

Tesla walked over to Claire. When he got close to her, he was so taken with her poise and beauty that he uncharacteristically faltered.

"I, I, want to apologize for, for the, the *cacophony* my assistant caused here this evening, Miss . . ."

"Claire LeFleur," she said. "Please, call me Claire." Li approached them, and Claire continued. "Your assistant didn't cause the cacophony, Mr. Tesla. Those louts were determined to ruin my evening long before you two arrived and . . ."

She looked at Li, smiled demurely, and added, "And saved me. My champions. Please, will you dine with me, or at least let me buy you a drink?"

She looked at the bartender, called out, "Bartender! Three glasses, please, and your finest whiskey."

The bartender replied, "Absolutely not! Not after what your friends did here. And certainly not the Chinaman! Now, out with the lot of you!"

He poured Smith a shot of whiskey and said, "Not you Major. Vets are on me."

Tesla said to Claire, "Thank you for your kindness, but as you can see, my assistant is rarely welcomed. Even in establishments like this, I'm afraid."

Li turned toward the door and said, "I need some air, Boss. I'll be outside. This place makes me sick."

"Wait, Mr. Li," Claire called to him.

Li stopped and turned.

Claire said to Tesla, "Since they won't have him, we'll all leave." She smiled coquettishly and added, "*Boss*."

As they walked toward the exit, through the war zone that was recently a bar, Tesla pointed at Moose lying there out cold, teeth missing, bloody knuckles and busted up head, leaned to Li, and whispered, "We agreed to be *inconspicuous*, Li. Do you call that inconspicuous?"

"No," said Li. "I call that unconscious."

A short while later, Tesla, Li, and Claire were perched on top of the oscillator pulse weapon on the barge, in the moonlight, sipping wine from stemmed glasses, and looking at the remains of Secretary Garrison's Cadillac. Soldiers were standing guard at the gate to the dock.

Claire looked at the dried blood on Li's wounded shoulder.

"You really should let me look at your wound," she told him. "It could get infected."

She moved closer to Li to inspect the wound beneath his shirt. He subtly pulled away and looked at Tesla, unsure, almost as if asking for permission.

"Well . . . maybe later, when the pain subsides," she said gently.

Sensing confusing tension in Li, she changed the subject.

"It really is quite a job preparing for war, isn't it? Besides learning all the medical equipment, we're being trained on what we might expect concerning casualties. War wounds are far different from common wounds treated in a hospital surgery. I learned that in the Red Cross. Among other things."

Li ignored her statement, asked her, "Where did you learn to speak Guāhuà?"

"I lived in China," she answered.

"North or southwest?" Li asked.

"North. Northwest of Tientsin."

"You lived all the way up on the Yellow Sea?"

Li thought for a moment. His smile began to fade.

He asked her, "Where north of Tientsin, exactly?"

"My father was stationed in Peking in 1899. He was a general."

"During the rebellion?" Li asked.

Claire nodded.

"I thought so," Li said.

He slid off the gun . . . and silently walked away.

Claire called after him. "But . . . Li? . . . Li, I—"

Li raised a hand behind him in dismissal. He leapt onto the dock and made a wide berth around a clutch of soldiers smoking cigarettes and sharing war stories next to the battered Cadillac. He walked slowly away, head down, mind churning, and disappeared into the shadows.

"What was that about?" Claire asked Tesla.

"I think you may have stolen poor Li's heart," he answered. "At least you may have, had you not told him your father might have killed some of his family in the Boxer Rebellion."

"In that case, more like broke his heart, then. That was not my intent. He asked why I was there. I told him the truth."

She moved closer to Tesla. Looked in his eyes.

She smiled. She was beautiful.

"I hope you won't hold that against me, too. Do you?"

Tesla broke her gaze, glancing down the pier in the direction Li had gone.

"I'm apolitical. I care more about helping people than about warring against them."

He turned back to her, smiled uneasily, and raised his glass.

"A toast," he said. "To you and the Red Cross. If there was a reason to believe in angels, it would surely be you. So . . . stay under the care of their wings and . . . fly home safe from the war."

They clinked glasses and sipped.

"You are certainly more romantic than your writings on gravity and electricity would suggest, Mr. Tesla," she smiled.

"You've read my writings?"

"Who hasn't?" her eyes dreamily sunk into his gaze. "The famous Mr. Nikola Tesla. The handsome Mr. Tesla."

She took his hand.

He hesitated.

"Romantic?" he said, pulling his hand from hers. "Romance would be a discovery far beyond anything I could imagine. I'm afraid I don't seem to find time for romance in my life. Too many things to discover. Too many people to try to help."

She looked away, hurt. He moved toward her, unsure, nervous, out of his depth.

"No, Claire . . . I didn't mean . . . you are a beautiful young nurse. Surely you must—"

She pulled away, cutting him off defensively, "I am not so young, Nikola. And why would you assume that I'm a nurse? In fact, I am a physician. A scientist, just like yourself."

A contrite look came over his face.

"Forgive me, Claire. That was insensitive of me—even sexist. I should never have made such an assumption. But . . ."

"But *what*, Nikola?"

"But I beg to differ with you."

She rose up, preparing to be indignant.

"About *what?*"

"You indeed *are* a beautiful young woman."

She coquettishly bit her lip, and smiled.

He smiled, raised his glass, and said, "To you: the beautiful, young, Red Cross doctor."

She raised her glass and responded, "And to you: the handsome, older, famous doctor."

"My doctorates, however, are honorary," he smiled. "Yours is real."

"Then, to the handsome, older, brilliant scientist."

They laughed and took a sip.

On the dock, in the dim moonlight, the shadowy form of Major Smith was barely visible, standing near the group of soldiers as they chatted among themselves. He retrieved a cigarette packet from his jacket pocket and lipped one. As the flame from his gold lighter touched the cigarette, his eyes were briefly lit by the glow.

And they were riveted to Claire.

CHAPTER 8

The Proposition . . . And the Warning

The following morning, a long, flatbed military vehicle, with the oscillator pulse weapon strapped down under a tarp, pulled into the gravel parking area in front of Wardenclyffe tower. The truck stopped, backed up, and parked at the front doors of Tesla's laboratory. Soldiers jumped out and took positions around the truck.

The lab door opened, and Tesla and Li emerged into the sunlight, striding toward the truck just as a military sedan drove into the yard and pulled in behind it.

Secretary Garrison and Major Smith got out.

"So much for a Chinaman's chance in hell," Smith called out as he and Garrison approached Li and Tesla.

Li ignored Smith entirely and walked past him to the flatbed.

Smith shot a conspiratorial smirk at one of the guards and said, "I see the little yellow bugger survived New London last night, eh?"

The guard glanced at Li, then back at Smith, and shrugged.

Tesla watched Li for a moment as he began helping the soldiers ready the gun to be unloaded from the truck. Then he turned and said to Smith, "Yes, he seems to have survived pretty darn well, hasn't he?"

He pointed at Smith's bruised cheek and added, "How's your face? Looks pretty nasty. Healing up all right, Major?"

"Just fine. Although I might need the services of your little nurse," Smith snapped.

"Actually, she's a doctor," Tesla quipped. "And I doubt she could do anything to help you."

Before Smith could respond, Tesla turned to Garrison and said, "Mr. Secretary. How nice to see you. I had no idea we'd be enjoying your company again so soon."

"Good morning, Dr. Tesla. We do have things to discuss."

"Obviously—as I see you weren't delivered here in your Cadillac Phaeton. I trust it was insured?"

"It was a government vehicle. Which brings up our problem from the test yesterday."

"Of course, Mr. Secretary," Tesla began, hands on hips as he watched the men carefully take the weapon into the lab. "Obviously, we now realize that there are things we didn't know about the physics of the device. When we have a chance to analyze and discern the problem, rest assured, we will solve it."

"I have every confidence that you will, Dr. Tesla."

Everyone reacted as the pallet carrying the gun hit the ground.

"Careful there, Li," Tesla called out.

"It's fine, Boss."

Garrison turned back to Tesla, subtly tapped his attaché case, and said, "Is there someplace we can talk, in private? I have a message. From President Wilson."

"Of course. This way."

Tesla led Garrison and Smith inside to a leather-appointed, dark wood-paneled den. He motioned them to a pair of chairs on the far side of a glass-topped coffee table and sat down across from them.

Secretary Garrison placed his attaché case on top of the table, opened it, and pulled out an envelope that was addressed:

To Dr. Nikola Tesla—Eyes Only:
PERSONAL AND CONFIDENTIAL.

Garrison opened the envelope, withdrew a paper from it, and handed it to Tesla. Across the top was emblazoned *The White House—Office of the President*.

"This envelope is addressed 'personal and confidential' to me only," Tesla said. "I assume *eyes only* means my eyes only?"

"Yours are the only eyes on it," Smith snapped condescendingly.

"We are aware of the contents, Mr. Tesla," Garrison said. "Obviously, the president discussed it with us in detail before he had it memorialized and requested that we give it to you."

"But it's not signed," Tesla said.

"President Wilson has given his explicit blessing, Mr. Tesla," Garrison said.

"But not his explicit signature?"

"As you can see, it's on *his* letterhead," Smith said.

Garrison said, "There's a political term, Mr. Tesla, called 'plausible deniability.' President Wilson is up for second term next year and plans to win the election by keeping America *out* of the war. I assure you, however, that we have his guarantee, both in commitment and in financial support, that we will help the Allies."

"But that's over a year away," Smith added. "The Allies will be overrun by then. I probably don't have to remind you, Mr. Tesla, that Kaiser Wilhelm will consume your beloved Serbia—where, as you know, this nightmare began—with *Serbian* assassins!"

Smith stopped and let that sink in as he glared at Tesla.

In a hard, tight voice, Smith said, "We want that gun!"

Garrison interjected calmly, "Now, now, Major, we're not here to—"

"Stop pussyfooting around, Mr. Secretary! Soldiers lives are being lost as we speak!"

Tesla said, "I understand, Major Smith, that both civilians and soldiers are dying. However, that *gun*, as you call it, is a loose cannon, little more than a time bomb, the failure of which is the very reason we are sitting here right now."

"It destroyed a submarine—under the water! We need that weapon."

"As you will recall, having witnessed the scene with some jubilation just yesterday, Major Smith, almost everything metallic in proximity of the pulse was destroyed—not just the submarine. Do we really want it to be used to inadvertently take innocent lives? Because that's just what it will do if it isn't corrected. It's important that you understand this."

Li stepped into the room, sat down next to Tesla, looked pointedly at Smith, and said in a mock Chinese accent, "Cadirrac. Frat as pancake. You understand, Amelican?"

Tesla stifled a chuckle and said, "Insensitively put, Li, but completely accurate. Look, Mr. Secretary, you of all people must realize that the thing simply needs some fine-tuning." He looked at Smith and added, "And you, Major Smith, must understand the folly of going off half-cocked when soldiers' lives are at stake."

Garrison nodded. Smith looked down at the table and shrugged in acquiescence.

Garrison addressed Tesla. "You are right, Dr. Tesla. Look, we are not here for the gun. Not in the final analysis, anyway. What we are really here for, what we need the most, is your help. Will you assist our allies in finding those damn German U-boats? They are taking lives by the thousands, sir. We can agree to leave the actual destruction of the subs to the men who do that sort of thing."

He glanced at Smith. Smith nodded, his eyes narrowed, lips pursed.

"It's what I do, Mr. Tesla," Smith stated flatly. "Like it or not, I am a warrior, trained to fight, to defend, to kill the enemy when necessary. And right now, Mr. Tesla, that is necessary."

Tesla thought for a moment. He looked at Li. Then at Smith. Then at Garrison.

Garrison said, "You will be working to defend the innocent, Mr. Tesla. Will you help us? Your contribution would be greatly rewarded. We're talking about a *lot* of money—money we happen to know you could use. If you're successful, there's no end to the gratitude and financial remunera—"

Tesla cut him off. "How much money are we talking about, Mr. Secretary?"

Garrison said, "Name your price. You could fire up this tower of yours. Send your signals all around the world. Or whatever that thing does. Hell, send signals to Mars for all I care. Buy the Waldorf-Astoria. Do whatever you want."

Garrison paused and then added, "I don't want to beg you, Doctor I don't want to pressure or bribe or blackmail you. But, from one American citizen to another . . . will you help the helpless? Those who are about to die, those who are dying even as we speak, need you."

"We could order you, you know," Smith said.

"Major Smith!" Garrison barked, glaring at the major. "That will be enough. We are not here to strong-arm Mr. Tesla. Do you not understand how counterproductive something like that would be? Think it through, man."

Garrison turned back to Tesla and said, "You could travel to England and take over their top secret sonar program."

"They have one?" Tesla asked, surprised.

"Well, they're trying. And under your guidance, they could. You would have the top scientists and all their research at your disposal. You would be the team leader."

Garrison pulled out two more envelopes and put them on the table in front of Tesla.

One was bulging with cash. From the other, he retrieved a ticket for first-class passage on a luxury ocean liner.

Garrison said, "First-class passage on the—"

Tesla cut in, "My assistant, Mr. Li, would have to accompany me."

Garrison pulled a second ticket from the envelope.

"Absolutely. I have booked third-class accommoda—"

Tesla interrupted him again.

"Mr. Li would also be traveling first class. Preferably in a suite adjoining mine."

Garrison shot a knowing look at Smith, pulled another ticket out of the envelope, and said, "I counted on that. I perceive you to be a man of honor, Mr. Tesla. Here is a ticket for first-class passage for Mr. Li, in his own suite, next to yours."

Tesla and Li exchanged looks.

Garrison said, "When there is peace in the world, your country and the world will forever be in your debt. What do you say?"

* * *

In Tesla's lab later that night, Li was packing a steamer trunk with laboratory equipment and instruments while Tesla absent-mindedly studied the tickets, tapping them uneasily in his hand.

He stepped over to the pulse gun, lightly touched various parts of it, testing bolts here and there, feeling metal joints, tugging at wires, and running his fingers over some of the damaged parts.

"Why so troubled, Boss?" Li asked.

"Something's not right, Li. Fifty thousand dollars in cash? And first-class passage on this ship, the," he glanced at the tickets, still in his hand, and read the name of the ship, "the *Lusitania*, no less—one of the most luxurious liners on the seas? And they didn't bat an eye about putting you in first class, in your own suite—which is truly commendable, of course, but . . . something doesn't add up. And I can't quite figure it out."

He accidentally bumped his foot on the steel-reinforced wooden pallet to which the pulse gun was bolted. He looked down.

Li said, "They left it on, Boss. Good base. Solid. It's got rollers, too, if we need to move it."

"No. No need to move it. Not with the breech welded shut. How bad is it?"

Li spun the wheel, unlocked the breech, and opened it, revealing the core, still alive and glowing with very small lightning-like flashes.

"HA!" Tesla exclaimed. "It's still working." He turned to Li and said, "I thought you said it had . . ." Then it dawned on him. "You were only protecting it from Smith getting his hands on it, weren't you?"

Li peeked inside the breech. He shrugged and grinned, feigning surprise, and said, "Hmm. How about that! It must have fixed itself."

Tesla smiled in appreciation. As he delicately removed the core, he said, "Thank you, my dear Li. But, unfortunately the core must be destroyed."

"Destroyed?! Not so hasty, Boss! You have years of your life wrapped up in this. Just because one experiment didn't work, doesn't mean you throw bathwater on the baby."

"Throw the baby out with the bathwater, I think you mean."

"There, see—you agree with me," Li grinned.

Li gently took the core from Tesla and added, "Leave it to me, Boss. You can't destroy this any more than I could. How about I put it somewhere safe?"

"No," Tesla said. "It must be destroyed, Li."

"I'll put it someplace you won't know about. Far away from here. That way, when you come to your senses . . ."

"I will destroy it, Li."

"Not going to get the chance, Boss. Just think of it as gone forever. Now we should get you to the Waldorf. Big day tomorrow."

Tesla thought for a moment. He looked at Li. He slowly nodded. “You might be right. You never know when it might come in handy.”

Tesla gathered a few things and took one last look at the de-cored pulse gun. Li bolted the doors and started to turn off the lights.

Tesla said, “You go on to bed, Li. I’ll get those. I have a couple things I need to do before I retire for the evening.”

“You got it, Boss. See you in the morning.”

Li departed.

Tesla opened a cupboard, pulled out a bottle of Cabernet Sauvignon, and poured a glass. Thought a second. Called out.

“Twain? Would you like a glass?”

“Love one, my boy,” came Twain’s voice from the den.

Tesla poured a second glass, carried the two glasses into the den, and sat down next to Twain who was relaxing on the sofa in front of the coffee table. He handed a glass to Twain. Twain nodded. They sipped. Tesla absentmindedly turned the tickets over in his hand, deep in thought.

“What’s on your mind, my friend?” Twain asked.

“Something’s . . . bothering me.”

“Conscience?”

“That core is inside a weapon capable of mass destruction.”

“You are between a rock and a hard place, my boy. It’s a brilliant invention that could do much good if used properly.”

“But with the military now involved . . . the odds of that have gone down to zero.”

“I would advise you to trust Li to deal with the core. He always has your best intentions in mind. And, who knows . . . God may have other plans for that particular invention.”

Tesla nodded and shrugged.

As he took another sip of wine, his eyes fell on a dire warning printed on the back of the ticket:

NOTICE!

TRAVELERS intending to embark on the Atlantic voyage are reminded that a state of war exists between Germany and her allies and Great Britain and her allies; that the zone of war includes the waters adjacent to the British Isles; that, in accordance with formal notice given by the Imperial German Government, vessels flying the flag of Great Britain, or of any of her allies, are liable to destruction in those waters and that travelers sailing in the war zone on the ships of Great Britain or her allies do so at their own risk.

—IMPERIAL GERMAN EMBASSY,
Washington, D.C., U.S.A.

Tesla took another sip of wine. His thoughts drifted to Claire.

CHAPTER 9

Lusitania: In Her Royal Majesty's Service

The following morning, May 1, 1915, on the New York Harbor passenger liner docks, Tesla and Li were at Cunard Line's Pier 54, reading the schedule.

Posted beneath the schedule was the same warning that Tesla had read the previous evening. Li read the warning and then turned to Tesla with a worried look.

"Boss, it says here, 'Travel at your own risk.' Says it's from Imperial German Embassy in Washington. Sounds serious, Boss."

"There is such a thing, Li," Tesla responded reassuringly, "called Cruiser Rules. Officially, it's known as The Declaration of Paris. It lays out the rules for battles on the high seas where skirmishes involve civilian vessels between the combatants. America, dear Li, is not one of those combatants. We are neutral. We are quite safe. Let's get on board."

They continued walking toward the passenger entrance.

"But Boss," Li continued his inquisition, "how can we be safe if there is war going on?"

"The rules call for the passengers and crew members of civilian ships to be safeguarded if the Germans are going to attack a civilian ship. The Germans are certainly not allowed to sink a boatload of Americans—that would be an absurd mistake for the Kaiser to make."

They rounded a corner. They slowed to a stop at the sight before them. Towering above, like an iron giant, was the bow of a picture perfect, multi-decked, magnificent ocean liner. With only one thing out of place: on the bow, a paint crew was blacking out the name *Lusitania*.

"Seven hundred and eighty seven feet long," Tesla said admiringly. "The German liners dominated the emigrant passenger trade for so long that the Cunard company decided to make this ship, and her sister ship, the *Mauretania*, faster, more luxurious, and more modern. This one was built with completely redesigned turbine engines, capable of running at twenty-five knots. Elevators, wireless telegraph, electric lights everywhere, a recirculating air-cooling system, and one and a half times as much passenger space than any other ship on the sea."

He looked at Li and added, "When she was launched in 1906, Li, she was the finest example of mechanical and electrical engineering construction afloat on any ocean in the entire world."

"You sound like a talking billboard, Boss."

"She is a beauty," Tesla said, smiling up at the behemoth ship. He pointed to the four tall smokestacks and added, "Look there, Li. "Four funnels means four turbine engines, which means four propellers—massive ones, too. Big as a small house."

As they looked up at the stacks, a paint crew on a rope and platform rig was blacking out the last of the red color on the final stack.

"Boss," Li said. "That warning back there said, 'Vessels flying the flag of Great Britain, or of any of her allies, can be sunk if they are caught in the war zone.' Boss, what about vessels with nothing painted on them? We're still going to England. That's still a war zone."

"Well . . . yes, Li," Tesla said, his assuredness starting to falter, "technically it is. But—"

"No, not *technically*," a voice behind them suddenly interrupted.

They turned to see Major Smith approaching them.

"*Actually*," Smith continued. "Though we declared ourselves neutral, we *are* entering a war zone. And, in fact, just this February, Germany announced that they will no longer adhere to the Cruiser Rules."

"Li," Tesla said, a hint of nervousness creeping into his voice, "remind me once again: why am I doing this?"

Li said, "Money, Boss. Big money."

"Then I fear I have joined the ranks of the capitalists. My honor is no longer at stake. It's gone."

The blast of a steam whistle cut off all talk as they reached the boarding gangplank.

"Time to board," Smith said.

As they went through the embarkation line, the agent looked at Li's first-class tickets and then looked at Tesla and Smith, as if there was some sort of a mistake.

"He's with us," Tesla said importantly.

"With him," Smith said, nodding at Tesla. "Not with me."

The agent stamped the tickets and they were waved through as hundreds of passengers streamed aboard, treading up the gangways while cargo was being loaded. Latecomers were snaking through the crowds, and well-wishers were waving their good-byes.

Tesla led the way up the steep ramp, with Li behind him, and Smith following Li.

Li said, "With all the money you'll be making, Boss, you can get so much lightning, you'll be able to shoot to the moon with it." He glanced down—snapped his eyes immediately back in front of him, and added nervously, "Just don't look down, Boss."

Tesla glanced over his shoulder at Li and then abruptly looked up and forward. Two decks above them, standing by a rail, he spied Claire talking with a group of nurses.

Tesla looked back at Li. But Li had already spotted her. And he was enjoying the view.

"Hmm," Tesla said, "I see I won't be the only one thinking about getting some lightning and shooting to the moon."

From behind them, Smith quietly observed Tesla and Li as they watched Claire.

* * *

Meanwhile, back in Tesla's lab at Wardenclyffe tower, three brawny persons, dressed head to toe in black and wearing black knit ski masks, were muscling the pulse gun out of the lab.

Their boots were military issue.

* * *

Back on the *Lusitania*, a rigid, very proper gentleman in a British Royal Navy uniform walked in front of Tesla as he was about to step onto the ship at the top of the gangway.

He extended a hand to Tesla and said, "Dr. Nikola Tesla, I presume?"

Tesla looked at the officer and looked down at his extended hand.

"He doesn't like strangers touching him," Smith said.

"Actually, no one," Tesla said.

The officer awkwardly withdrew his hand and said, "Oh . . . well . . . jolly good, then. Welcome aboard. I'm Colonel Cornwell. His Majesty's Royal Navy."

"Thank you, Colonel," Tesla said. He waved a hand at the dozens of people on the steep gangplank behind him and added, "Is this where I ask your permission to come aboard, or do we have everyone wait whilst we chat?"

"Oh, yes, yes, sorry," Cornwell said, standing aside.

Li stepped onto the deck, followed by Major Smith.

Smith said, "Colonel Cornwell is my British counterpart. Same basic duties."

"Ah," Tesla quipped, "another U-boat killer, ey?"

“I wouldn’t put it that way, my good man. Seeing to *your* comfort and safety is of international concern. Anything you might need Doctor, Major Smith here and I are at your disposal.”

Smith nodded at Li, saying dolefully, “This one’s in first class too.”

Li extended his hand. Cornwell hesitated a moment, threw a quick glance at Tesla, and then grasped Li’s hand and gave it a hearty shake.

Smith gritted his teeth and looked away.

“Excellent, very good,” Cornwell smiled, adding, “I suspect we’ll all be best chums by the time this journey is over.”

A realization overcame Tesla.

He turned to Smith and said, “Am I to understand you will be traveling with us?”

Smith put on a prim smile and replied, “Oh, I wouldn’t miss this for the world, Mr. Tesla. Not for the world.”

Cornwell waved an arm ahead of him and indicated a doorway labeled *First Class Passengers Only* and said, “This way, gentlemen.”

Smith hesitated, threw a quick glance of disdain at Li, and followed them onto the upper decks of the majestic ocean liner.

Down on the pier, gangways were being pulled back, steam whistles were blasting, and crowds were biding cheerful farewell to family and friends.

Just above the waterline, near the ship’s stern, one last piece of cargo was being carefully loaded into an open steel cargo hold door: a single wooden crate with *PERISHABLE* stamped in big block letters all over it . . . just about the size of Tesla’s pulse gun.

With one long blast of the foghorn and thunderous cheers from the crowds on deck and on the dock, the monstrous, six-deck *Lusitania* was maneuvered slowly out of her berth by two tugboats.

Dozens of small boats, sailboats, motored launches, and yachts flanked the big ship as she steamed out of the New York Harbor, glided past the Statue of Liberty, and floated out to sea . . . two mortally crucial hours behind schedule, due to a last-minute transfer of forty-one passengers and crew from the ocean liner SS *Cameronia.*

* * *

Meanwhile, by means of wireless intercepts and radio direction location courtesy of the Royal Admiralty's tracking team known as "Room 40," the British Navy had been following the movements of a certain submarine named "*U-20*," commanded by a Kapitänleutnant Walther Schwieger.

Less than forty-eight hours earlier, *U-20* had departed its berth on Borkum Island in Lower Saxony, northwestern Germany, on a northwest heading across the North Sea. Loosely plotting a course for Peterhead while awaiting orders from German High Command, Schwieger had plans to proceed around the north of Scotland, and then to Ireland, to do some "opportunity scouting" along the western and southern coasts before entering the Irish Sea from the south.

Kapitänleutnant Schwieger and his crew were hoping for a little luck.

And luck was on the way.

CHAPTER 10

DINNER WITH THE CAPTAIN

In his luxurious stateroom on board the *Lusitania*, Tesla turned from admiring the view out the porthole to examining his suite. Lace curtains, ribbons on the pillows, plush couch, settee, overstuffed reading chair, and a green felt-shaded brass lamp on the coffee table.

"Greyhound of the Sea, hmm," Tesla murmured, nodding appreciatively. "More like the Waldorf on the water."

Just then, the door to the adjoining room opened and Li leaned in from his suite.

"Steamer trunks are here, Boss," he said. "Where do you want yours?"

Tesla waved him in. Li entered, followed by a black porter lugging a huge trunk on a trolley.

Tesla pointed at a floor-to-ceiling mahogany armoire and said, "Just park it there. I'll unpack it. Thank you."

The porter offloaded the trunk from the trolley and then hovered near the door, a pleasant smile on his face as he looked expectantly from Li to Tesla.

Tesla patted his pockets and said, "Ah, yes—your tip."

Just then, Major Smith treaded in from Li's room.

"Mr. Tesla," Smith said. "I thought I heard your voice. I saw Li's door open and—"

"Ah, Smith," Tesla cut him off. "Just in time. Tip this good man, will you? I'm a little light on cash at the moment."

Smith looked from Tesla to the porter to Li.

Li suddenly found something urgent under a fingernail that needed his attention and began to studiously pick at it while quietly whistling "Dixie."

Smith shook his head tersely, pulled a silver 25¢ piece from his vest pocket and jabbed it at the porter.

The porter looked at the coin. Looked at Smith. Shrugged. Dragged his trolley to the door, muttering under his breath, "Ok, well . . . I guess if that's all the man can afford up here in first class, then . . ."

The porter opened Tesla's door to exit, and Colonel Cornwell was standing there in mid-knock. The porter attempted to bypass Cornwell as he entered the cabin.

"I'll collect that from you later," Smith groused at Tesla about the tip.

"I seem to have found the party," Cornwell said, smiling and stepping aside to let the porter out.

Cornwell came into the suite, looked around, and said admiringly, "Very nice. I trust this is up to your standards?"

Li said, "Eh. It's a little small."

"A little *what?*" Smith said, trying to maintain his composure. "Used to better, are you?—it's practically the damn presidential suite."

"Li is right, actually," Tesla chimed in. He looked at Cornwell and added, "We'll require a laboratory of sorts. Seven days sequestered at sea is far too much valuable time to be wasted floating in a boat."

"Doesn't have to be a huge space," Li added. "Something out of the way, preferably. A workbench. Adequate electric power—which means a good deal of electricity, if you can spare it."

Tesla glanced surreptitiously at Smith and threw in, "And a *locking* door would be nice, as well."

"Of course, Dr. Tesla," Cornwell said. "I'm sure we can accommodate all of that. And we will, of course, make sure you remain uninterrupted during the journey. Now, let's allow you gentlemen to get settled."

Cornwell looked at Smith and indicated the door.

"Oh, one more thing before you leave," Tesla said. "I would like to have a look at the research to date. As soon as possible, if you don't mind."

Cornwell and Smith exchanged puzzled glances.

"Research?" Cornwell said.

"Notes, experiments, findings?" Tesla responded.

Cornwell shook his head and shrugged.

"You do have something for me from our British counterparts, correct? Schematics? Blueprints?"

After observing their uneasy glances at each other, Tesla said, "Gentlemen. Please. I assure you, we are no strangers to secret projects. They will be safe with us here until we secure a space. After all, I believe it was the president of the United States who approved of our liaison through the secretary of war, was it not? You do understand the meaning of the word *liaison*, I assume?"

"It means *cooperation*," Li said, grinning at Cornwell and Smith.

Just then, there was a knock on the door. Li moved forward to open it. A trio of stewards was standing there bearing fancy floral arrangements.

Li pulled the door wide and stepped back. The stewards entered the suite.

The chief steward handed an envelope to Tesla and said, "Compliments of Captain Turner. This is his personal invitation, Dr. Tesla."

Tesla opened the envelope, pulled out an ornately embossed card, and read it aloud: "'At the personal request of Captain William Thomas Turner, you are hereby cordially invited to attend a private executive tour of the *Lusitania*, followed by cognac, whiskey, wine, and cigars in the first-class parlor, which will be followed by dinner at the captain's table.' It's signed: 'Captain William *Bowler Bill* Turner.'"

Tesla handed it to Li, saying, "I assume this nickname indicates his preference for bowler headgear."

Li nodded and muttered, "Sounds like," as he read the invitation himself.

Smith looked at Li like he wanted to throw him overboard.

Tesla looked at Cornwell and said, "What became of Captain Daniel Dow? I thought he was commander of the *Lusitania*."

“Captain Dow was under a lot of stress from navigating sea lanes that have been swarming with increased German submarine activity,” Cornwell responded. “So Cunard Line Chairman Al Booth had him take some leave time.”

Smith said, “And Dow was wrongly complaining that the *Lusitania* had become an armed merchant cruiser and thus a prime target for the U-boats. Which, as an employee of Cunard, was none of his concern.”

“Is she an armed cruiser?” Tesla asked Cornwell.

Smith said, “I hardly think that’s—”

Tesla cut him off and continued speaking to Cornwell. “I understand that the British government paid for much of the *Lusitania*’s construction under the condition that, if necessary, she could be easily converted into an armed merchant cruiser.”

“An auxiliary cruiser, Mr. Tesla,” Cornwell countered. “There’s a difference.”

“I further understand,” Tesla went on, “that when this abominable war broke out, the Lusitania was requisitioned by the Admiralty as an AMC and indeed was listed officially as such, along with her sister ship Mauretania.”

After an awkward silence, Cornwell responded, “I can neither confirm nor deny that, Mr. Tesla.”

“Besides,” Major Smith added, “that is really none of your concern, is it, Mr. Tesla?”

“It is, actually, Major Smith,” Tesla replied. “In that, as Britain’s new scientific partner in this venture, it would be nice if my partners would be honest with me about various crucial elements of the enterprise upon which we are embarking together.”

“What ‘crucial elements’?” Smith asked.

“Such as, how much danger we are in—danger about which you are not telling me, your partner, and about which you apparently have no intention of warning hundreds of other innocent passengers.”

Before either man could respond, Tesla looked at the chief steward and said, “Please inform Captain Turner that my assistant Li and I will be honored to accept his invitation.”

Smith said to the steward, “And make sure that the captain understands that not only are our distinguished guests VIPs, but also they are under *my* protection as a representative of the United States government, as well as under the protection of Great Britain.”

Tesla shot an annoyed look at Smith and then said to the steward, “I'm sure the captain will extend the invitation to include our *military* escort as well.”

Tesla pulled a $5 gold coin from his inside coat pocket and held it up in front of the chief steward.

Both the steward's and Smith's eyes went wide at the sight of the gold piece. Smith's jaw clenched as the steward held out his hand.

Tesla dropped the coin into the steward's outstretched palm and said, “You will see to it that Captain Turner understands my wishes, won't you, my good man?”

The chief steward grinned widely. “Oh, yes, sir! I will let him know, sir! You can count on me, Mr. Tesla.”

Tesla turned and addressed the room: “Now, gentlemen, it's feeling a bit like the Brooklyn IRT station in here. If you don't mind, we would like to have a little time for rest and relaxation before we dress for the tour and dinner with Captain Turner.”

The stewards exited the suite.

Smith glared at Tesla and growled, "I thought you said you were broke!"

"Broke? *Me?* My dear Major Smith, I'm Nikola Tesla. I'm hardly broke. Especially not compared to that miserly tip you gave to that poor porter. Now, if you gentlemen don't mind."

He padded to the door, opened it, and stood aside.

Smith and Cornwell eyed each other a moment and then looked at Tesla. Cornwell gave Tesla a short bow, turned, gave one to Li, and he and Smith stepped out.

Li watched them as they padded down the plush carpeted first-class corridor. Li closed the door after them and turned the deadbolt. He leaned his forehead against the door dramatically, as if the weight of the world had just been lifted from his back, and said to Tesla, "Why did you have to invite *him*, Boss? I'd rather row this tub to England myself than spend another minute in his company."

Tesla said, "There's an old saying, Li: keep your friends close, and your enemies closer. There's no better way to keep an eye on them than to let them think they're keeping one on us."

Li faced Tesla and said, "I've got a saying, too, Boss: just because a snake can smile, doesn't mean you should pet it."

Tesla glanced at Li, trying to fathom what the heck that meant, then shook his head in puzzlement and deadpanned, "Li . . . go unpack."

* * *

A short while later, Smith and Cornwell rendezvoused at the stern's second-level rail. Smith leaned on the rail and watched as the sea behind the big ship churned the wake into three rows.

Cornwell opened an engraved silver cigarette case, rapped it upside down against his fist, shook out a cigarette, and offered it to Smith.

"Murads," Cornwell said. "Turkish. Hand rolled."

Smith nodded, slid it out, and pumped it in his mouth. Cornwell lipped one, struck the lighter to Smith's and then to his.

Smith took a long drag, blew it out, and said disgustedly, "What right does Tesla have to question the intentions of the British Admiralty concerning this ship?"

Cornwell flicked some ash and replied, "He seems to know an awful lot about the ship, doesn't he." He looked at Smith and added, "Why don't you find those stewards and warn them not to spread any of Tesla's claptrap about the ship being an armed merchant cruiser. I'll have a talk with Captain Turner later about Tesla's . . . *attitude*."

"Good idea," Smith said. He thought a moment and then said with a hearty chuckle, "A *laboratory*, with a lock, he said—on the outside, no less! Couldn't have been better if I'd planned it myself."

"He's pretty sharp, Major," Cornwell said. "Wonder what the odds are that he'll catch on."

"He honestly believes his hands are clean. I suggest you come up with some of the research he asking for, Colonel. Or a damn good reason why you don't have it."

Cornwell looked at him and smirked. "All we have is rubbish, Major. Our scientists have come up with nothing. Absolutely nothing. Tesla is light-years ahead of anyone in this field. Hell, he *is* the field. What's your plan once he figures out he's being used?"

"We always allow for, uh . . . *contingencies*, Colonel," Smith replied ominously. "Obviously he's not as smart as he thinks . . .

'*With a lock,*' he said! That one killed me! He'll be in his own padded cell."

Cornwell said sternly, "It is absolutely unacceptable to the Admiralty to, to . . . practically *kidnap* Nikola Tesla. We won't be locking him up, Major. It's against propriety and decorum. Besides, he's too well known—we'd never get away with it."

"You'll change your tune if he figures out what's going on. Until then, he'll feel secure. And he's free to roam about. Within reason."

"Does he even know it's on board?" Cornwell asked.

"Of course not."

Cornwell blew a thin stream of smoke. After thinking a moment, he looked at Smith and said, "It would not surprise me if you Americans had some other plan up your sleeves, under the pretext of—"

"*War*?" Smith spat. He flicked his cigarette off the fantail with an angry thrust and added, "Under the pretext of *your* war, Colonel Cornwell. You cried out for America's help and when we offer it, you throw *decorum* in my face? If you had seen what I saw when Tesla tested that thing on a metal building in New York City, Colonel, you would grasp this immediately: the nation that controls that weapon, wins the war. And the world."

Cornwell took a deep pull on his cigarette. He savored the taste and exhaled slowly. Then he looked at the cigarette.

"Turkish tobacco," he said. "Smoothest in the world. The Turks killed us like flies on a swatter in Gallipoli. Now we can't get enough of their smokes. 'The world turns,' my dad used to say." He flicked the butt over the rail and added, "But I will blow my brains out with my own Webley .455 automatic before I am forced to eat even one mouthful of sauerkraut." He turned to

Smith and said, "You're right. Do what you must, Major. Do what you must."

* * *

Two hours later, as the top rim of a purple sun slowly dipped below the misty horizon, the VIP tour was concluding. The small group walked toward the entrance to the first-class smoking lounge, led by Captain Turner, a thick man with a square face and the piercing eyes of an experienced sea captain. Turner was engaged in conversation with a man on his right, Alfred Vanderbilt, tall, aristocratic looking, in his late thirties, sporting a natty moustache and dressed in a stylish, hand-tailored suit and polka-dot tie.

"Her engines can pull 68,000 horsepower—three times stronger than Dreadnought-class battleships," Turner was telling Vanderbilt, "and one and a half times more powerful than the Invincible-class battle cruisers."

"All very good and well, Captain," Vanderbilt responded. "These are prosperous times for America, supplying our friends across the pond. War is money, money is power, and together, they know no bounds."

"My dear Mr. Vanderbilt, for the next week, let's try to forget this damnable war," the captain said, patting Vanderbilt on the back. "Think of the *Lusitania* as an oasis. Your private island in a sea of peace."

"Captain, please," Vanderbilt said. "I hardly see these seas lurking with peace."

"Alfred, Alfred," Turner said. "This ship is indeed a safe haven for many neutral nationalities. It would not be in Germany's best interests to even think of trying to sink the *Lusitania*. Besides, she is much too fast for the U-boats."

Tesla was walking on the other side of the captain. As the group reached the entrance to the lounge, Tesla turned to Captain Turner and pointed to the fourth smokestack, which had no smoke billowing out.

"But Captain," Tesla commented, "is the *Lusitania* fast enough to outrun a German submarine with only three of her four boilers fired?"

The group stopped as Captain Turner looked up at the empty funnel.

He took a breath and said, "Astute observation, Mr. Tesla."

The captain addressed the guests behind them: "Those of you who may have stood on the aft deck and observed our departure from New York earlier might have noticed that there are only three wakes being created by the *Lusitania*'s steam engines. This is because, while the ship has four turbines—one to drive each propeller—boiler four is currently on reserve because coal is a precious commodity during wartime, and we do our part to conserve. So I assure you, ladies and gentlemen, even with only three boilers lit, this ship will still be able to outrun any German sub."

Tesla leaned over to Li and said under his breath, "If we can *see* them, that is. But if we can't, then even with engine four fired up too, we're sunk, my dear Li. *Sunk*."

"Yes, Dr. Tesla?" Captain Turner said. "Did you say something?"

"No, no. Just commenting that what you said was, uh, no bunk. The efficiency of the turbines is a little less at lower speeds, but they do gain significantly more power with the engines at all ahead full."

"That's correct. No submarine can catch us."

Vanderbilt looked at the captain and deadpanned, "I didn't expect a mad dash through an armed gauntlet to the Isles, Captain Turner."

"We'll be fine, Mr. Vanderbilt." Turner indicated for the group to follow him inside and said, "Let's go inside now, ladies and gentlemen, and enjoy an apéritif and appetizer before dinner."

They stepped into the magnificent first-class lounge. The room was capped with a stunning, barrel vaulted, twenty-foot, stained-glass dome, the skylight of which had twelve stained-glass windows that each represented a month of the year.

The lavish, nearly seventy-foot-long room was walled in inlaid mahogany panels that surrounded yellow floral patterned jade green carpeting. The room was elegantly furnished, decorated in Georgian style in satins and leathers. At each end of the room was a fourteen-foot-high green marble fireplace adorned by enamel panels, the design of which flowed over onto the decorative plasterwork.

A wide selection of kir, vermouth, brandies, and dry wine were on display, spread across dark, polished wood tabletops, along with a dazzling display of appetizers.

Turner stopped and addressed the group. "Please, take a few moments to enjoy the finest canapés, caviar, Cuban cigars, brandies, or wines."

Vanderbilt retrieved a cigar clip from a pocket in his waistcoat, selected a Cuban with a dark wrapper, and was reaching for a cigar lighter when Tesla came over to him and held up a small high-tech-looking device vaguely reminiscent of a cigarette lighter.

"Allow me, Mr. Vanderbilt," Tesla said.

Vanderbilt put the Cuban cigar in his mouth and leaned toward Tesla's hand, and Tesla pushed a lever on the side of the lighter. As the top of the device clicked open, a tiny, blue-white bolt of electricity flickered between two bronze points.

Vanderbilt pulled back in surprise.

"It's okay," Tesla smiled. "Just put the end in the middle of the arc there."

Vanderbilt leaned his cigar into the electricity. The cigar instantly began to smolder. Vanderbilt eyes went wide with delight as he puffed the end of the stogie's leaf to a glow in the spark.

"Another one of your futuristic electrical inventions, Dr. Tesla?" Vanderbilt said and smiled appreciatively as he blew a stream of blue smoke toward the ceiling.

Tesla nodded. "It is I who stand in the presence of fame," he said. He gave a slight bow and snapped the lighter shut.

"Well, fortune maybe," Vanderbilt responded. He gave Tesla a small bow as well and added, "But it is you who are the famed one, Mr. Tesla."

"It must feel very . . . odd to be the wealthiest man on the planet," Tesla said.

"Only in the Americas, as far as I know. But all I do is make money. You make a difference."

Vanderbilt poured two brandies and handed one to Tesla. Tesla passed it to Li. Vanderbilt poured another and handed it to Tesla.

"Mr. Vanderbilt, I'd like you to meet my fellow scientist and trusted colleague, Li Yín Huŏ."

"My Chinese is a bit rusty," Vanderbilt said. "But isn't *yín huŏ*, what . . . metal and fire?"

"Very good," Li responded. "Almost. It actually means silver and fire. I like to think of myself as bright as silver and fearless as fire," he added with a grin.

"And I like to say silver fire is simply electricity," Tesla quipped.

"Touché!" Vanderbilt said. He raised his glass and added, "Welcome aboard, Li. It is a pleasure to make your acquaintance."

From across the room, Major Smith and Colonel Cornwell observed the grinning trio as their brandy glasses clinked.

An hour later, dinner was being served in the first-class dining room, an ornately decorated, two-tiered area with Romanesque columns, white walls, and gold filigreed wainscoting and molding in the style of Louis XVI.

The captain's large, round table was positioned on a raised level overlooking the room. Seated with the captain, sharing food, wine, conversation, and laughter, were Tesla, Li, Smith, Cornwell, Vanderbilt, Elbert Hubbard, and Charles Frohman.

"Mr. Hubbard," Captain Turner said, "where is your lovely wife Alice this evening?"

"Working on another book," Hubbard said, adding with a chuckle, "But you know these women's rights activists today—don't be surprised if she's busy organizing your female workers into some sort of collective at this very moment."

The men laughed.

Vanderbilt said to Charles Frohman, "How very much I enjoyed, *Peter Pan*, Mr. Frohman." He said to Tesla, "Mr. Frohman here is a most accomplished Broadway producer."

"So I understand," Tesla said, nodding to Frohman.

"Good gracious," Frohman replied to Vanderbilt. "But that play was a decade ago."

"And yet," Vanderbilt responded, "if a U-boat were to try to sink us today, you could probably just up and flitter away like Pan."

"Eh. U-boats are the least of my worries," Frohman responded drolly. "It's the floating IOUs from the theaters that concern me."

The men chuckled.

"Gentlemen," Turner said, "should the *Lusitania* come into harm's way from U-boats, we have learned much since the sinking of the *Titanic*. For instance, we have more than enough lifeboats and life jackets to go around."

"That'll be helpful if we run into an ice pack," Tesla said.

The men laughed.

Hubbard said, "If there's a German submarine in these waters and they find out I'm aboard, they'll punch holes in this ship like Swiss cheese."

More laughter.

Vanderbilt said to Tesla, "Mr. Hubbard published that scathing commentary depicting the Kaiser as a monster lusting for blood."

"So I read," Tesla replied. "Nice to know that if we're sunk, at least we can blame it on Mr. Hubbard's penchant for invective whilst we sit in our abundant lifeboats awaiting rescue, passing wine and cheese."

The men all roared.

Only Major Smith seemed not to be humored by the conversation.

A steward whispered in Captain Turner's ear. Turner nodded, stood, and tapped his glass for attention. The room quieted.

"Ladies and gentlemen," Turner announced to the room. "You have already probably noticed the smartly uniformed young women sitting at some of the tables among you."

Guests turned and noticed a few nurses sitting with other guests at various tables.

Turner continued. "These women are from hospitals all over America. They have very graciously and bravely volunteered their services to assist Great Britain and our allies with the harrowing task of tending to the many casualties of this war. Will you please join me in saluting the commitment and courage of these beautiful young nurses."

Everyone stood and loudly applauded. The nurses stood and smiled in acknowledgment of the appreciation. As the applause died down, the nurses sat down. Only one woman remained on her feet: Claire LeFleur.

Claire looked at the captain and addressed the room: "With the captain's kind permission, I wanted to say that, as a point of fact, while we are all beautiful, we are not all nurses. Some of us are doctors."

The men were clearly taken by the outspoken young Claire. Li, still harboring ill feelings about her father's profession in China, couldn't hide the fact that he was more than taken by her poise and beauty; he was enchanted.

As Claire's eyes caught Li's, Major Smith looked from her to Li and back, as he studied them both.

Turner said to Claire, "Are you a doctor, Miss—?"

"LeFleur. Dr. Claire LeFleur," she replied. "At your service."

"Please," the captain said, "will you come and join us up here at my table, Dr. LeFleur?" He turned to the steward and said, "Bring her place setting over here and another chair for the doctor—and a glass of Champagne."

Claire excused herself from her table and walked to the table up front as the guests returned to their meals. She reached the captain's table. All the men stood.

She was seated next to Tesla on her right, Captain Turner on her left, and Vanderbilt directly across from her. She acknowledged Li and the others and held her smile on Vanderbilt a bit longer as Turner lifted his glass in a toast.

"To our beautiful young *doctors*, as well," Turner said.

They raised their glasses demurely and lightly tapped them together.

Claire raised her glass and said, "Over the teeth and past the gums, look out stomach, here it comes!" then tossed back her Champagne in one gulp.

The men laughed and took a drink.

Claire nodded at Tesla and Smith, saying, "Mr. Tesla. Major Smith." She looked at Li and added, "And my dear Mr. Li." Then she turned to Vanderbilt and said, a hint flirtatiously, "And the nonpareil Mr. Alfred Gwynne Vanderbilt. I am so very pleased to meet you."

Vanderbilt became a bit flushed, smiled, took a quick sip of his drink, nodded, and waved off the attention. "The pleasure is mine, Dr. LeFleur."

"You've met?" Captain Turner asked Claire.

Claire replied, "Not everyone. But certainly, Mr. Tesla, Major Smith, and Mr. Li are my heroes. They rescued me from certain bodily harm—and who knows what else."

Tesla said, "I assure you, gentlemen, I had no part in this clever young lady's rescue. Unless heroic is tossing a pool cue to my assistant Li in the heat of battle—which he then used to dislocate the jaw of one of Dr. LeFleur's attackers."

This bawdy revelation was a bit of a surprise to the group at the table. Smiles faded. Glasses were silently lowered. Throats were cleared.

"I was there, gentlemen," Smith said, breaking the silence. "It was a regular donnybrook."

"Saved my life, the major did," Li said.

Smith gave only a prim smile in acknowledgment of the compliment.

Li turned to Claire, saying, "I'm sure the good doctor is no stranger to men vying with fisticuffs for her attention."

"Gentlemen, please," Claire said admonishingly. "Let's behave."

"Speaking of fighting with a woman present," Turner said, "tell us, what is expected of you? How close will you be to the front? And why in God's name would you volunteer to embark on such a dangerous assignment?"

Claire looked around the table. Her eyes stopped on Smith and Cornwell, in their military formal dress whites.

"Duty. Love of country," she said. "And the fact that I'm a terrible cook, I can't even conceive of trying to raise a child, and I'm not queasy at the sight of blood." She put a hand on Tesla's and added, "And, like Mr. Tesla here, I don't mind getting my hands dirty."

Tesla glanced uneasily at her hand on his—a discomfort that Smith casually noticed.

"Well then," Vanderbilt said, looking around at the other men, "you're in good company. There's not a clean hand in this bunch."

As they each smiled and murmured with varying degrees of enthusiasm, Tesla used the diversion to slip his hand from under Claire's. She glanced at him. Smith and Li watched.

"My Boss's passions are discovery and invention," Li said. He looked at Claire and added, "His loyalties lie with one mistress only: science. My question to you, Dr. LeFleur, is, where do yours lie?"

"In helping make this a better world."

Li commented, "Ah . . . that, coming from the daughter of a general who assisted in slaughtering Boxers like my father, is reassuring."

The comment elicited awkward silence at the table.

"Li," Tesla said, "Claire can hardly be held accountable for her father's actions or his choice of careers."

"I can defend myself, Mr. Tesla," Claire said. She turned to Li and added, "It is true, Li, that my father fought the Boxers. But that was because the Yihetuan Movement threatened the lives of both foreigners and Chinese Christians alike. But, as Nikola said, I am not my father. In fact, I was only a teenager of nineteen when the rebellion ended in the fall of 1901. Li . . . we can choose our friends, but we can only hope that those who could make us their enemy would choose *not* to do so."

Their eyes locked for a moment. Li broke her gaze, looked down at the table, and murmured under his breath, "Yes . . . I would hope they would have that ability."

"Elegantly put, Dr. LeFleur," Vanderbilt said. "I myself cannot recall ever choosing an enemy. But I seem to be pretty damn adept at making them, for some reason."

Their tablemates erupted in laughter, relieved that the awkward moment had passed.

Only Smith remained unmoved.

* * *

Two hours later, in his suite, Li heard a knock at the door. Li slid open the peep door to see the perfectly framed face of Claire.

He hesitated as they looked at each other.

Sensing his reluctance to open the door to her, she said, "Think of me as an on-duty doctor." She smiled and bit her lip coquettishly. "And you as a patient whose shoulder was recently cut in a bar fight by a guy as big as a moose. Over me. And you won."

That broke the ice. Li fought off a smile.

Claire smiled and added seriously, "If you don't let me dress that wound, it will get infected if it's not already. With a good seven days before we reach a real hospital, I suggest you let me in to tend to it. Or get used to the name Lefty."

He closed the peep door, unlocked the door, opened it, and stood aside to let her in.

Claire walked in, carrying a medical bag. She looked around and nodded toward a stuffed chair.

"Sit there," she told him.

He sat on the chair.

"Take off your shirt."

He looked at her hesitantly.

"If you don't remove your shirt, how can I play doctor with you?" she smiled cutely.

The look on his face changed to alarm.

"Oh, calm down," she chided him. "I'm only joking." She rummaged in her bag and pulled out a pair of scissors. She scissored them open and closed and then added with a grin, "Now get that shirt off before I cut it off."

Li let out an exasperated breath and said, "Are all female doctors this annoying?"

"Only the ones who operate on stubborn Boxers."

He shot her a look.

"I'm joking, Li! *Sheesh!* Are all Chinamen this grumpy?!"

He shrugged out of his shirt. She carefully cleaned, sutured, and bandaged his wound, her soft fingers occasionally touching here and there. She stopped to check her work. She leaned in. Her silky hair touched his face; her red, perfect lips touched his shoulder. His breathing sped up. He closed his eyes. She bit off the end of the suture.

He said, "Hudnut. Three flowers."

She leaned back, took the stitch from her mouth, flicked it away, and said, "What?"

"Your perfume. It's Three Flowers. By Hudnut."

A smile slowly overtook her face as she looked at him.

"I'd like to come," she began in a soft, nervous voice; then she paused and said, "—I mean . . . if you're good, I can . . ."

She stopped. Took a breath. Took a step back. Gathered her thoughts. They looked at each other a moment, imaginations running wild.

She pursed her lips, blew out a stream of breath, said, "Okay. Let me try that again. What I'm trying to say is that this dressing should be changed regularly. I can come and do that for you. And if you're a good healer, I can remove the stitches before we reach Ireland . . . Whew."

Li grabbed his shirt, started putting it back on, and replied, "I'll be fine. But thank you. For all that."

She helped him into the shirt, saying, "That's fine, too. I'm sure Mr. Tesla will help you if you—"

"Mr. Tesla isn't comfortable around anything unclean."

"He considers you unclean?"

"No. Blood. Germs. Bacteria. That sort of stuff."

"Nikola is an odd man in some ways, isn't he? The more I learn about him, the . . . well, the farther away I feel from him."

"He lives mostly in his head. He's always thinking, analyzing, calculating, imagining, creating."

"That makes sense. He's a scientist, an engineer."

"But he's also a poet and a philosopher. A walking contradiction, you could say."

She sat on the padded arm of his chair. "And what about you, Li? Why did you come to America?"

He looked up at her. His eyes narrowed. He said menacingly, "I came to find the man who killed my father."

Her jaw dropped. Her eyes went wide.

"Gotcha," he grinned. "Just joking."

She rolled her eyes.

"Actually, I had no choice," he said. "I came to America and was sold as a laborer to pay off my passage from China."

"Like slave labor?"

"Hard work, but I'm used to it. I never felt the hate that many of the others did, because I wanted to come and I agreed to the terms. Only by sheer will have I learned not to lose my honor. Mr. Twain gave me the drive to learn to read. I learned your language, your customs, even your religion. By the time Mr. Tesla won me from Mr. Twain, the debt was paid and I was a new man."

"If the debt is paid, why do you keep working for Nikola?"

"Because it's Nikola Tesla," he said. "The most famous and brilliant man on the planet today. Besides, he treats me as an equal, a peer almost. He teaches me science and engineering. So, I serve him, and he takes care of my living expenses."

"What a beautiful story. Nikola found a true friend in you, Li. One he stands up for and believes in."

"And I in him. I also had a friend in Mr. Twain. He was the first white person to give me hope for all white men. Because of him, I believe in America. He was a great man. He was a Boxer at heart."

She took Li's hand. He started to pull back. She gripped it tighter and said, "Trust me."

He relinquished. She placed his hand on her chest.

She said, "I hope, one day, that you discover that I too am a Boxer at heart. For I already consider you a friend."

After five seconds that felt like an hour to him, Li pulled his hand away. They looked at one another a moment. She stood and gathered her bag.

"See you around. Lefty."

She walked to the door, opened it . . . and floated away.

He closed his eyes, breathed her scent deeply in through his nostrils as she disappeared down the hallway, and whispered, "See you around, Three Flowers."

Outside the porthole window, the moon bathed the tips of the choppy ocean waves like snow on mountain peaks as the mighty liner steamed her way . . . to destiny.

CHAPTER 11

Schemers

It was day two in the British Parliament war room. Cigar smoke blanketed the air like a layer of London fog as a heated argument wore on between Winston Churchill, Prime Minister Herbert Asquith, Admiral of the Fleet John "Jacky" Fisher, and War Secretary Kitchener.

"Rules!?" Churchill barked at Admiral Fisher. "You bring up rules, when it's the Germans who are barbarically slaughtering our troops! How is *that* following rules!?"

"That doesn't mean that we, too, sink to the lowest common denominator along with them, Winston," Asquith said. "We are still civilized men."

"And uncivilized brutes will rule us if we do nothing!" Churchill thundered, slapping a heavy palm on the tabletop. "We need America in this war! And, Prime Minister, if that means American lives must be lost, then so be it! What part of that equation escapes you, sir?!"

There was a silent pause as the implications of what Churchill was suggesting registered with the assembled leaders.

Fisher broke the silence. "We cannot afford to have the Americans realize too late that if Germany conquers Europe . . . the United States is next. It would only be a matter of time."

"President Wilson is doing all he can to prevent that from happening," Asquith remarked.

"Wilson is doing *nothing*," Churchill groused, lighting another cigar. "All he chooses to make are piddling little moves calculated to appease his church-mouse constituency while ignoring the advice of his own war cabinet." He blew out a gob of smoke, squinted through the haze, and added in a gravelly rumble, "I am getting very tired of saying this, gentlemen, but until there is American blood in the water, every so-called helpful gesture of theirs will be *meaningless*."

"Winston," Asquith responded, "the more determined Wilson is to stay out of the war, the more their arms shipments to us increase. For that, we should be grateful."

"Grateful?!" thundered Churchill. "I'd be grateful if they'd stop pussyfooting around, grow a pair, and act like real men! What do *you* suggest, Prime Minister, for convincing the Yanks to help us, for God's sake? Beg on our bloody knees? Then, fine!—I, for one, will beg on my bloody knees!"

A uniformed officer entered, handed an envelope to Asquith, and retreated from the room. Asquith tore open the envelope, ripped out the letter, briefly scanned it, and then handed it to Kitchener.

Asquith addressed the men smugly. "There actually are new efforts afoot to aid us, gentlemen." He nodded at Kitchener.

Kitchener read aloud from the letter: "'The bird is on the wing.' Signed, '*Lusitania*.'"

Churchill drew hard on his cigar and blew out the smoke with a look of skepticism on his square face.

"Tell him the rest," Asquith told Kitchener.

Kitchener addressed Churchill. "There's a scientist. His name is Tesla."

"Nikola Tesla?" Churchill said. "The Slav?"

"Actually, he's Serbian. An electrical engineer. Quite brilliant. He has invented a secret . . . super weapon of sorts."

"Super weapon?!" Churchill barked. "Didn't he sell some of his engine patents to Germany? How can we trust a man like that?"

"That was well before these hostilities," Asquith said.

"I hear Tesla is a madman who can't be trusted," Churchill grumbled. "The only *super weapon* we need to save Britannia is one we already have: His Majesty's Royal Navy. Most powerful military force on the planet."

"Fine," Asquith shrugged. "Then you won't mind doubling the escorts when the *Lusitania* enters the war zone . . . just in case Tesla is not the madman you claim him to be and actually might have a weapon we can put to good use."

* * *

Meanwhile, that same afternoon in France, gathered in the ornate war room of the French government, hunkered down in well worn, dark leather chairs, French Prime Minister Aristide

Briand was talking with three men: Chief of Staff of the French Military Marshal Joseph Jacques "Papa" Joffre, sporting a sweeping, white moustache; Tzar Nicholas II, last Emperor of Russia, a trim, elegantly bearded man; and Russia's Minister of War Vladimir Aleksandrovich Sukhomlinov, a bald man with a white goatee.

Briand was fidgeting nervously. Tzar Nicholas was stirring tea in a delicate porcelain cup. Vladimir Sukhomlinov was pacing, his boots stomping with each step. Marshal Joffre was slouched in a thick-leathered chair, his squinting eyes taking in every gesture and word as each man spoke.

"Every day," Nicholas said, "our combined forces grow weaker, while the Germans become stronger. We must get the Americans into this war—by any means necessary."

"Such as?" Vladimir asked.

"Such as putting a US ship on the bottom of the Atlantic!"

"Don't count on your mad cousin Kaiser Wilhelm to sink an American ship, Nicholas," Joffre said. "Not even he is that insane."

"Maybe not," Nicholas replied. "But that doesn't mean the crazy old bastard can't be blamed for an . . . *incident* that might result in the loss of American lives."

"I take it you are referring to the *Lusitania*," Vladimir said. "She left New York yesterday, May 1, at noon, with 200 Americans on board. She is scheduled to enter the Irish Channel on May 6."

"And?" Briand coaxed. "What of it?"

"We have a certain . . . agent on board," Nicholas said. "A man of German origin."

"A German?" Briand said. "Why not French? Or Russian? Of all nationalities, why German? If he's even remotely suspected, why—"

"*If* he is caught," Vladimir said, "it will only convince the British that crazy Kaiser Wilhelm is behind it. But if he's not caught . . ."

"Behind *what*, exactly?" Joffre asked. "What have you got planned?"

"A bomb," Vladimir replied. "We all know what contraband they carry, even passenger ships. Once *Lusitania* enters the war zone . . . *Boom!* The bomb goes off, and the *Lusitania* goes to the bottom."

"A bomb," Briand deadpanned. "Are you as mad as the Kaiser? How big is this bomb?"

"It doesn't matter how big or small it is!" Nicholas blurted. "What matters is that Mother Russia—along with all the other countries—will join together in accusing Germany of the merciless U-boat attack that killed . . . as many Americans as it will take to get them into this war!"

"Are you insane as well?!" Briand stated. "Murdering innocent Americans and pinning it on the Kaiser to force President Wilson into action?!"

Nicholas faced Briand and asked him, "Would you prefer, Prime Minister Briand, to teach your children to learn to speak German?"

The room went silent.

* * *

Meanwhile, in the war room of the German High Command, Hugo von Pohl, Commander of the German High Seas Fleet, addressed Kaiser Wilhelm and Grand Admiral Tirpitz: "We have confirmed that the so-called super weapon—the one the

Americans call the 'sub slayer'—and its inventor Nikola Tesla, are en route to Ireland aboard the *Lusitania* at this very moment."

Wilhelm scoffed in disbelief.

"Sub slayer?" Tirpitz barked. "What the hell are you talking about?"

"It split a Dutch submarine right in two," Pohl exclaimed.

Wilhelm rolled his eyes and chuckled. "They're buckets! Holland knows nothing about building U-boats. Theirs are toys compared to ours. I could split one in two with a German steel hatchet."

"If I may speak freely, Herr Kaiser," Tirpitz said. "Underestimating Nikola Tesla may not be wise. I am convinced that, at all cost, we must prevent the delivery of this device to the British. Our total, crushing victory could depend on it."

Wilhelm thought a moment and then said, "Then sink her. End America's neutrality. Put the *Lusitania* on the bottom."

"But . . . sink a passenger liner?" Pohl said.

"We did not make up the Cruiser Rules, and we've already issued a warning," Wilhelm replied. "Let the world know this: Germany means what Germany says!"

"Our agents on board have suggested another plan, Herr Kaiser, a *better* plan," Tirpitz interjected.

"Such as?"

"Cripple the liner with a torpedo. During the mayhem and the rescuing of passengers . . . we offload the weapon onto our submarine."

A smile spread across Kaiser Wilhelm's face.

"We spare the passengers," Tirpitz continued, "the Americans are not harmed, and the United States continues to stay out of the war."

Pohl added, “We show both compassion *and* bring the weapon to the motherland.”

“Brilliant!” the Kaiser crowed. “We look like heroes to the world—neither England nor America would ever admit they’d had a weapon stolen from under their noses—they’d look like fools! I love it!”

“Also, if possible,” Tirpitz added, “we bring Tesla to Germany. If half of what they report about him is true, having Nikola Tesla—this ‘sub slayer’—to do our bidding . . . why, Germany could develop the world’s ultimate weapon.”

Wilhelm stood. “Who is our most distinguished U-boat captain?” he asked. “We will send him to the *Lusitania* at once.”

“That would be Kapitänleutnant Walther Schwieger,” Pohl responded. “He is headed for the north of Scotland as we speak, mein herr. Awaiting orders.”

CHAPTER 12

ORDERS

Kapitänleutnant Walther Schwieger, a baby-faced young man of thirty, with short red stubbly hair, a well-trimmed beard, and steel gray eyes, gripped the handles of the periscope in the *U-20*. He carefully placed one eye to the scope. His other eye squinted closed as Schwieger's steady, perfectly manicured fingers precisely fine-tuned the viewfinder.

Four crewmen, bathed in an eerie red glow, stood dead silent at their stations in the sub, resting less than twenty feet beneath the surface of the frigid North Sea.

Above, on the surface of the sea on the western side of north Ireland, a British Royal Navy destroyer was steaming south.

Beneath the waves, on board the *U-20*, Schwieger spoke softly to the man standing next to him, Torpedo Officer Raimund Wiesbach, a short, bespectacled man with a broad, prominent nose.

"Four remaining?"

"Yes, Captain," Wiesbach whispered.

"Target acquired," Schwieger said quietly to a crewman seated at a control panel. "Stand by, torpedo one."

"Target acquired," the crewman repeated into a com tube. "Stand by for torpedo one."

"Arm torpedo two," Schwieger said.

The crewman repeated the order into the tube.

"Steady," Schwieger said. "Steady . . . fire one!"

The crewman repeated the order to the tube room, waited a second, and then said, "One away, Captain."

Schwieger's eye was glued to the image in the periscope as a stream of bubbles marked the path of the torpedo three feet below the surface of the water as it speared its way toward the destroyer.

"Three . . . two," Schwieger whispered as he watched the scene in the periscope, " . . . one—*contact*."

The words left his mouth the instant the deadly bubbles stopped and—*BOOM*!—the torpedo struck the destroyer mid-ship, forcing it to bend upward in a violent geyser of water and heavy debris.

Captain Schwieger lifted a hand to his well-disciplined crew to silence them should some initiate a premature celebration.

In the scope, Schwieger observed the merchant vessel the destroyer was protecting emerge from beyond the crippled and quickly sinking destroyer and enter the crosshairs.

"Fire two!" Schwieger called out.

The crewman relayed the order, waited a second, and then said, "Two away, Captain."

"Three . . . two . . . one—*contact!*"

BOOM!—the sub was rocked by the two massive successive shockwaves from the explosions as torpedo two struck the merchant ship dead-on.

Schwieger snapped the periscope handles shut, lowered the scope, and turned to Wiesbach.

"Now we celebrate. Then we head back home to refuel and take on more torpedoes."

The crew let out a loud cheer and prepared to take *U-20* to the surface.

Schwieger turned to Wiesbach, saying, "Take us up. Prepare to man the deck gun. Ready a crew for salvage operation."

"Aye, sir," Wiesbach said.

On the surface, the front of the *U-20* burst out of the water like a whale shark and settled with a thunderous crash onto the sea. In the distance, the sinking ships were ablaze, with seamen scrambling to lower lifeboats and survivors scurrying to the sides and leaping into the freezing water even before lifeboats were safely away from the mortally wounded vessels.

The hatch on the *U-20* swung open. Schwieger clambered up the ladder and stepped onto the deck. He stood next to the conning tower, raised his binoculars, and scanned the wrecks.

Wiesbach climbed up the ladder and onto the deck with a piece of folded paper in his hand.

"Decoded, mein Captain," he said, handing Schwieger the note.

Schwieger let the glasses hang around his neck, took the note, opened it, and began reading.

Wiesbach looked at the mayhem barely a hundred yards away as survivors of the targets rushed to make it into lifeboats.

He stepped to the deck machine gun, racked it, and said to Schwieger, "Permission to fire, sir?"

Schwieger turned abruptly from the note and barked, "Nein! We sink ships. We do not kill unarmed sailors. What's our fuel?"

"Low, sir. Enough to make it back to Bokrum. Not much more."

"Tell the men there will be no salvage operation."

"We have enough fuel for that, sir."

"I said there will be *no* salvage operation, Mr. Wiesbach," Schwieger repeated firmly.

"Aye, sir."

"Torpedo count is two?"

"Yes, sir, two fish left. It's been a good run. The crew will be glad for a break."

Schwieger looked down at the note in his hand without lifting it to read. He slapped it twice against his thigh, saying distractedly, "Yes, it has been. Dismissed."

"Aye, sir," Wiesbach saluted. He started back to the hatch.

"Oh, Mr. Wiesbach," Schwieger called after him.

"Aye, sir?"

"Tell the men there will be no shore leave when we get to base. We take on diesel and weapons and go right back out."

"Sir?"

"Just tell them."

"Aye, sir."

Wiesbach stepped slowly down the hatch ladder, with a puzzled expression on his face.

Schwieger took one more look at the decoded note in his hand . . .

Mission bestätigt. Gehen Sie 190 kilometer südwestich von Fastnet Rock, vor Südspitze Irlands. Sie werden die Lusitania begegnen. Erwarten signal von kontakt. (Mission confirmed. Proceed south 190 kilometers southwest of Fastnet Rock, off southern tip of Ireland. You will encounter the Lusitania. Await signal from contact.)

* * *

A few degrees south and several miles to the west, as dusk settled over the Atlantic Ocean, the lights of the magnificent luxury liner began sparkling to life . . . like diamonds sprinkled across a black velvet casket.

CHAPTER 13

SPIES

Later that night, in the cargo hold of Bulkhead 51, a hot, cramped space with steel walls and a heavily riveted bulkhead door, Tesla was hard at work on a sonar wave detector test model on a metal table. Papers were strewn across the desk, penciled edge to edge with equations, rough-drawn schematics, measurements, and diagrams.

Tesla was focused on the test model, which was resting in the middle of the table on top of all the papers. The contraption looked very much like . . . well, like what it actually was: two standard tin pouring funnels pointed in opposite directions, as if for sending and receiving sound.

Seated on a wooden shipping box near the table was Mark Twain. White suit, white mane, white moustache. Mischievous eyes.

"You know, they do have their uses," Twain was saying. "They can be quite helpful."

"They're thieves," Tesla responded. "Time thieves. And I have no time to spare as it is."

"Ah, yes. So many of them, so little time for them."

"The problem is, the more attention one pays to them, the more they require."

"*Demand*, is more like it," Twain chuckled. "But they do have their . . . finer points, Nicky. And that one is quite fetching, I must say."

Just then, someone banged on the door.

Outside in the musty corridor stood Li and Claire. Li pressed an ear to the steel door.

"What is it?" Claire asked.

"Shh!" Li said. "He's talking to someone—there's somebody in there with him."

"But . . . who?"

"Boss!" Li called out. "It's us. Me and Claire. Are you in there?"

Inside the makeshift lab, Tesla quickly covered his test model experiment with newspapers and turned some documents and blueprints facedown.

He looked at Twain for a moment, confused.

"I'm no problem," Twain smiled. "I doubt they'll even see me."

"Right. Probably not."

Tesla padded to the door, leaned in, and said, "Is that you, Li?"

"Yes, it's me, Boss," Li said from the other side.

“Ah, Li. Hold on a second.” Tesla said.

He started to turn the steel wheel to open the door.

“And me. Boss,” came Claire’s voice.

Tesla stopped turning the wheel, his eyes squinting in thought.

“Uhh . . . can I help you?” Tesla called out.

“What do you mean *help me*?” Li said. “I work with you. Remember? Little Chinese guy? Kicks ass? Protects the women?”

Claire giggled.

Tesla said, “Yes, I understand all that. But what are you doing? I’m kind of in the middle of something here.”

“You don’t have a girl in there, do you?” Claire asked, adding jokingly, “*Again?*”

“Boss, we’re supposed to have dinner with Captain Turner. Remember? I checked your room but you were gone. Are you ready to go?”

Tesla looked at the ceiling, shook his head in annoyance, and glanced at the crudely constructed test model on his bench.

“Look, Li, I’m sort of at a critical phase here.”

Twain said, “Oh, open the door. She won’t bite you. I’m telling you, women do have their finer points.”

Tesla thought a second. Raised his hands in submission. Called out toward the door, “Okay, okay. Just a minute, Li. Be right there.”

He quickly made sure everything was covered up and swung the big door open.

Claire instantly burst in, looking around.

“Who were you talking to, Boss?” she asked smiling cutely. She spied the newspapers covering a lump of something on the bench, asked, “What are you building?”

"You may stop the *Boss* routine now," Tesla said. "That's Li's domain."

He placed a hand on the newspaper-covered experiment and shot a look at Li.

"Vanderbilt got Claire a seat at the captain's table," Li said.

"For the *entire crossing*," Claire added.

"Oh . . . that's . . . wonderful. I'm sure," Tesla responded unconvincingly.

"Then you do it," she said. "Nothing more boring than talking with the driver of this big tub every single dinner. And lunch. And breakfast."

Tesla looked at Li and asked, "Do you suppose the captain would be greatly offended if I beg off tonight?"

"Fat chance, Doc," Claire said, taking Tesla by the arm, grabbing Li's arm, and spinning them both toward the door. "Do you suppose *I* would be offended if you beg *me* off tonight? Besides, somebody's got to chaperone tiger Li here."

Tesla had no choice. As Claire traipsed them out the door and into the corridor, Tesla looked at Li and mouthed, "Tiger Li?"

Tesla locked the heavy Bulkhead 51 door. And half an hour later, they were sitting with the captain in the first-class dining room.

* * *

Champagne was flowing at the captain's table. Claire was seated between Captain Turner and Vanderbilt. Tesla, Li, Smith, Cornwell, Frohman, and other guests were also sitting at the elegantly appointed table, along with Hubbard, who was in the middle of a long-winded discourse . . .

"When I say this particular war is one of manipulation fueled by greed," Hubbard was saying, "what I mean is that the blood filling the trenches and battlefields—from both sides—flows through the same aristocratic European bloodline. Their so-called animosity is more akin to feuding siblings."

"Siblings with large armies and money enough to wage wars, yes," Tesla stated.

"It is telling of their character that the combatants in this horrible war are Queen Victoria's children and grandchildren," Li said. "Privileged classes that never had to work because they inherited their wealth don't seem to understand who it is that fights and dies for them—for a pittance."

Cornwell's jaw clenched. Smith eyes narrowed at Li's outspokenness. Tesla nodded in agreement.

"So true," Claire said. "And if they're fortunate enough to escape death, the physical ravages of war often make the rest of their poor lives a nightmare. Still, many soldiers do fight for honor and for their nation."

"And others fight because they're forced to fight the wars started by the so-called royal classes," Li added. "Like Tsar Nicholas the second. And that crazy Kaiser Wilhelm. And—"

"At any length," Cornwell cut in with a forced smile and a raised glass, "that train has left the station and all we can do is ride it to its destination. I want to propose a toast to all those in harm's way. And to us for a safe voyage."

"Here, here," Vanderbilt nodded and raised his glass.

They all joined the toast.

"Captain Turner," Claire said, turning to the head of the table, "tell us something we don't know about the *Lusitania*. Something fascinating. Maybe even something scandalous."

"Yes," Frohman said. "Such as, what sort of contraband are we sitting on?"

Captain Turner's face became serious. He looked around the table.

"Something juicy," Claire said. "Something we'd never guess in a million years."

Just as Turner was about to speak, a steward approached and handed him a note. Turner read the note—and suddenly his eyes went wide and he inadvertently blurted out: "Spies on board!?"

Smith and Cornwell shoved away from the table and stood. All eyes shot to the captain. Smith grabbed the note from his hand and read it.

Turner stood and said, "If everyone will please excuse us."

Smith handed the note to Cornwell and said, "Possibly they're only stowaways. If not—"

"We'll find out in short order," Cornwell finished Smith's sentence as he read the note.

"Probably stowaways," Frohman said. "Considering the cost of passage on these floating hotels."

"Captain Turner," Smith said. "Take us to where these men are being held." He turned to the table and added, "The rest of you stay here."

Vanderbilt said, "Not on your life, Major. I came for a first-class adventure and I'm fearless enough to have one."

Smith said, "Nobody's going but us. Not until we know what we're dealing with."

Vanderbilt waved him off, stood, and said, "Bosh. Safety in numbers, I say." He looked at Tesla, asking, "What say you, Nikola? On for a little adventure?"

Smith stomped out of the room muttering vague complaints about disobedient millionaires. Cornwell and Turner strode quickly out behind him.

Frohman said to Li, Claire, and the rest of them, "May as well drink up. They'll be back before desert."

Claire scooted a couple of chairs nearer to Li and said, "You may have to protect me all over again."

* * *

Deep in the bowels of the ship, a uniformed security officer and a short, stout man were padlocking three rough-looking men together with a length of chain to a steel bar in the floor of an iron-walled hold just as Turner, Smith, and Cornwell hurried in.

"Is that them?" Turner asked.

The man turned and answered in an Irish accent, "That they are, Captain. Three of them. Krauts, all."

Turner looked at the Irishman, saying, "You look familiar. You're in first class, aren't you?"

"I am, sir. Of sorts. Detective Inspector Bill Pierpoint of the Liverpool Police, at your service."

"I don't recognize the name."

"I'm traveling under disguise, sir. British Intelligence received a tip about one of your former crewmembers, British fellow by the name of Neal Leach, tutored Germans in English before the war. Washington notified us that when Leach arrived in America, he met with German agents. We've been on his tail ever since. We think he was involved in secreting these men on board."

Turner said, "Why wasn't I informed of this?"

"You just now were. Sir."

Just then, Vanderbilt strolled in, followed by Tesla.

The security officer standing guard over the three suspects addressed Cornwell. "They haven't said a word since we grabbed them, Colonel."

Cornwell spoke to the biggest prisoner. "Who are you, man? Tell me your name."

The prisoner sneered and grunted in response.

Smith shouldered past Cornwell and gave the man a hard kick to the gut. The prisoner groaned and doubled over in pain but refused to cry out.

"Speak, or I'll really give you something to groan about!" Smith snapped. "Now, who are you?! Where are you from?"

Captain Turner pulled Smith back, saying, "I'll not tolerate beating these men, Major, saboteurs or not."

Smith shook Turner off, barked at the prisoners, "I am a US Army Intelligence officer. Colonel Cornwell and I will be the judge and jury here in these matters." He turned to Turner and added, "You just pilot the boat, Captain Turner." Looking back to the prisoners, he asked, "Is it true—you're all German?!"

They said nothing. He kicked the big one again—leaned down and punched another one in the face.

Turner said, "Major Smith!"

Smith ignored him and bellowed at the prisoners, "Who are you!?"

"They wouldn't tell us if they were spies anyway!" Turner addressed Smith angrily. "Stop hitting them, immediately—what if they don't understand English!?"

"Then try this," Smith barked at the prisoners, "*Sagen sie mir! Sind sie Deutsche*?!" (Tell me! Are you German?!)

He grabbed the collar of the one he hadn't yet hit and raised his fist to strike him—the man cringed, nodded quickly, wagged a finger between all three of them, and said, "*Ja! Ja!* German!"

"Bloody hell!" Cornwell yelled. "They're Germans!"

"And fools for getting caught," Smith said and slammed the man back to the floor.

Turner said, "Well . . . they're locked up now. And they're going nowhere until we reach port."

Smith smoothed a hand over his hair, shook out his sleeves, looked at his knuckles, and said, "Maybe a little solitary will loosen their tongues."

He stared down at the three. He spat at them, barking, "If not, a fist in the face will be the best of what you'll be getting!"

"Gentlemen," Turner said, "the show is over. They're in custody now." He turned to the security guard. "Put four men on them, round the clock."

"Yes, sir."

Turner addressed the group. "Let's get back to dinner, shall we? We have plenty to talk about over brandy and cigars."

As they treaded out of the hold area, Vanderbilt leaned to Tesla and said, "It's turning into a trip to remember, eh Nikola? And we're only three days from entering the war zone, where things might really heat up."

"How lovely," Tesla replied tersely.

* * *

Later that night, Smith and Cornwell were checking on the crated oscillator pulse weapon and inspecting the rear cargo hold where it was resting.

"No signs of tampering," Smith said.

"No evidence of intruders, either," Cornwell responded.

"Well . . . hopefully nobody knows it's here."

"What if the damage is already done? How would we even know it?"

"Can't ask Tesla," Smith replied. "He doesn't even know it's here—and we can't let him know, or he'd put up a stink."

"Who's to say those three were the only spies on board?" Cornwell asked.

"That's why I'm here," Smith responded. "Because I trust no one." He looked hard at Cornwell and added, "Do you understand me, Cornwell? *No one*."

As it dawned on Cornwell that Smith was including him on his distrust list, he remarked, half under his breath, "My God, man . . . you're quite mad."

"Oh, you don't know the half of it."

CHAPTER 14

Echoes of Madness

Early the next morning, Tesla was pacing, deep in thought, on the bow just below the upper deck. Children were scampering to and fro around the curved walls of an alcove, their voices bouncing and echoing as they laughed and played.

Occasionally, a child would come running at him, and he would have to swivel out of the way. As he walked, he began to notice that the sounds of the children laughing and clapping were bouncing off the walls in different ways.

He stopped abruptly. He listened intently. He backed one slow step at a time into the curved alcove. He moved out of the alcove. In. Out. He smiled.

"That's it!" he cried out.

He looked at a wooden bench near the rail, where Twain was joyfully watching a little boy about six years old playing nearby.

"Twain, I've got it!" he said.

Facing the curved wall, he backed toward the railing, counting off paces and sharply clapping his hands every few steps. Halfway across the deck, he glanced at the deck above and saw Smith and Cornwell standing at the rail, looking down on him in utter puzzlement. Tesla nodded at them, continued backing up toward the rail, clapping every few steps.

When he reached the rail, he turned, glanced down, and saw Claire and Li standing together on the deck below.

As he turned to back up again and recount his paces to the curved alcove, he saw Cornwell and Smith watching them all. He smiled at them and made his way toward the curved alcove, stopping and clapping every few paces. The children followed him, clapping along with him.

"What game are they playing?" Smith sneered as he and Cornwell watched Tesla and the giggling kids following him. "The pied piper?"

As Tesla reached the alcove, he waved Twain over to him.

Smith and Cornwell looked at the empty bench Tesla was waving at and then back at Tesla.

Cornwell shook his head slowly and said sadly, "That poor chap is crazier than you, Major."

CHAPTER 15

INTO THE WAR ZONE

That night Li and Claire were standing in the corridor outside Tesla's Bulkhead 51 lab, pounding on the heavy steel door. On the floor in front of the door were two trays of uneaten food.

"Boss, come on," Li called out. "Open up. We know you're in there."

Smith and Cornwell came tromping around the corner.

Smith looked at the trays and asked, "What's going on? Is he all right?"

"Is he in there?" Cornwell asked.

"He's there," Li said.

Smith shouldered Li aside and pounded on the door. "Mr. Tesla?!" No response. He pounded harder, yelled louder, "Tesla! Open up or we'll be forced to—"

The door opened a crack. Smith stopped pounding.

"Do you mind?" Tesla said. "I'm busy here."

Cornwell said, "Mr. Tesla you cannot simply lock yourself in your laboratory and refuse to eat. We are responsible for your safety. I must insist that you make yourself available to us at all times."

"I do not need babysitters nor am I required to *report in*, Colonel Cornwell."

"But you do need to eat, Boss."

"Li's right," Claire said. "You haven't touched a thing."

Smith looked at Li and said, "It's your job to see that Mr. Tesla is looked after."

"I do have other things to do, too, you know," Li snapped defensively.

"Such as what—chase this innocent young lady all over the boat?!"

"Oh, I'm hardly innocent, thank you," Claire shot back at Smith. "Besides, how do you know who's chasing whom?"

"Young lady!" Cornwell said, scandalized.

Their bickering was abruptly interrupted by a loud electrical feedback sound suddenly piercing the air from inside the lab.

Claire jammed her palms over her ears.

Smith instinctively reached inside his jacket for the pistol in his pit holster.

Cornwell yelled at Tesla, "Good God man—*what is that!?*"

Tesla looked at them calmly for a moment, his eyes moving from one to the next . . . and the noise suddenly stopped.

"In light of the fact that you have not provided me with one shred of research from the British counterparts I was supposed to have received help from," Tesla said, "I call it progress."

Oddly, Tesla's voice was sounding, but his lips weren't moving in synch.

Smith shook his head, blinked a few times, and said, "Say again?"

Cornwell's eyes were glued to Tesla's lips.

"I said," Tesla's voice announced—although his lips weren't moving, and when they did, they were again out of synch with what he was saying: " . . . that I haven't had much—"

Li grinned and said, "That's not ventriloquism, folks."

"What in tarnation!?" Cornwell exclaimed.

Smith raised his hand, calling out, "Not another word!"

Tesla said, "I couldn't agree more."

They all looked from Tesla to the sound of his voice echoing toward them from down the metal corridor behind them. Yet, no sound was coming from his mouth.

"Now if you will excuse me," he said.

This time, the echo of his voice was coming from the opposite end of the corridor. Smith, Cornwell, and Claire were turning in all directions in confusion. Li was grinning.

"Good night," Tesla said. "I have work to finish."

He slammed the heavy steel door shut and turned the wheel.

They stood there, looking at each other like witnesses of a UFO who were too embarrassed to admit it.

Inside the lab, Tesla turned from the door, grinned at Mark Twain, and shook his hand vigorously.

Back out in the hallway, Li, Claire, Smith, and Cornwell were still standing there.

"Should we be concerned?" Cornwell asked Li.

"Yes you should—the minute you stop believing in the brilliance of Nikola Tesla."

Li bent down, picked up the food trays, and handed one to Claire. They padded down the corridor and disappeared through an exit.

"I've got my eye on that yellow dog," Smith said.

"Apparently, so does that little trollop," Cornwell responded.

"Hopefully, we'll get that curious sonar thing—or whatever it is—from Tesla too. As a bonus."

* * *

Meanwhile, as their third day at sea melted into the fourth, and the fifth into the sixth, Tesla worked feverishly on his sonar wave detector in his lab. Sometimes Twain was there. Sometimes he was who-knows-where in the universe.

Sometimes Li assisted Tesla. Sometimes he was "busy" with Claire . . . putting up little resistance as his budding friendship with Dr. LeFleur grew from puppy love and blossomed into romance. And didn't stop there.

In the meantime, Major Smith and Colonel Cornwell trained. A mix of Greco-Roman wrestling and boxing. Smith would rather take a knife in the eyeball than lose. Cornwell was more gentlemanly. Both revealed themselves to be adept at hand-to-hand combat. Smith won more often than Cornwell, but Cornwell didn't seem to mind.

The *Lusitania* continued steaming steadily east by northeast, headed for Ireland.

Baby-faced Kapitänleutnant Walther Schwieger continued putting ships on the ocean floor, taking nearly three dozen to their watery graves thus far.

Churchill and the British War Cabinet continued arguing over the best way to drag the Yankees into the fray. Churchill continued to act with his customary brash rudeness, behaving as if someday he would become prime minister.

The German War Cabinet continued tracking the *Lusitania* on their giant wall maps and tabletop ocean models.

Smith and Cornwell took to playing chess, grousing about the scandal "that damn Tesla's Chinaman" was causing with "that damn woman doctor" while they played. Cornwell generally checkmated Smith, but Smith didn't seem to mind.

Whenever Li would assist Tesla in the lab, Claire would bring them their meals, and the three of them (four if you counted Twain—although he wasn't always there) would lock in, eat together, share intense conversation and good wine, and increasingly, Li and Claire would take the food trays to "return them to the dining room" and then disappear for the entire night while Tesla continued working into the wee hours of morning, as was his custom, usually falling asleep on a portable bed he had commandeered from steerage class.

Each morning, Li would enter the lab at sunrise, pull a blanket over Tesla's shoulders . . . and puzzle over the two brandy glasses . . . one nearly empty, the other always full . . . on opposites sides of the makeshift coffee table next to the rollaway bed. Li assumed Tesla had received a visit from either Smith or Cornwell at some point during the night, to be grilled or admonished or whatever it was military officers did on a ship at sea with no soldiers to square away.

Li assumed wrong.

* * *

At dawn on the sixth day of the crossing, Tsar Nicholas asked Minister of War Vladimir Sukhomlinov an interesting question: "*Vy uvereny, chto oni dazhe ne podozrevayut yego*?" (Are you certain they do not suspect him?)

"*Da, da, opredelennya*," (Yes, yes, certain.) Vlad nodded vigorously.

"*Oni vkhodyat v zonu zavtra*." (They enter the zone tomorrow.)

"*Da. Ya znayu*." (Yes. I know.)

At that same moment, on board the *Lusitania*, a suspicious character was observed lurking about. The man was tall, well built, sported a blond bristle-top haircut, and had blue eyes. He also happened to be on the wrong end of a furious chase underway in the lower deck corridors and bulkheads, barely keeping ahead of Colonel Cornwell, who was huffing and puffing but keeping up the pressure on the running blond man.

The blond man hurried down a corridor, slipped suddenly left, slid through a bulkhead door, missing being seen by Cornwell by a less than a second, and kept racing pell-mell down the corridor.

The blond hugged the shadows. Got his heaving breath under control. Let his eyes adjust to the sparse string of low-wattage overhead bulbs. He set out at an easy trot, down stairways, more twist and turns, and soon found himself at the end of a corridor in front of a locked cargo hold door.

He grabbed the big steel wheel, pulled hard to the left with all he had in him. He stopped suddenly, strained to listen . . . heard Cornwell's boots on metal stairs, closing fast. He threw his weight into the wheel. It slowly twisted. He opened the door . . .

slipped inside . . . closed it quietly. But not quietly enough—it squeaked to a stop. He froze. He heard pattering footsteps running past the door and fading down the hallway.

He waited.

The footfalls returned.

He remained statue still in the pitch-dark hold. He put his hands carefully, quietly on the wheel, gripped it tightly in place.

Just outside the door, Cornwell stopped to catch his breath. He examined the heavy door. He tried the wheel.

In the hold the blond held the wheel fast.

Out in the corridor, Cornwell put all his bulk into it.

The blond was stronger. He heard Cornwell's footsteps fade away.

The blond fished in his pockets, retrieved a box of wooden matches. Struck one and saw in front of him: hundreds of cases, all marked *BUTTER—KEEP REFRIGERATED*.

He pried back a board on a box. What he saw was not butter.

"Ouch!" he cried out as the match burned down to his finger and thumb—but not before he caught a glimpse of the shiny brass tips of scores of 76-millimeter fragmentation shell casings.

He struck another match, carefully made his way deeper into the hold, and spied thousands of smaller boxes. He pried one open. It was brimming with Remington .303 rifle cartridges. He looked around at the countless boxes and let out a low whistle.

"Must be *thousands* of shells here," he whispered, adding, "*millions* of rounds."

He looked around the room again, found a lantern by the door just as his second match burned out. He grabbed the lantern and lit it. He shrugged out of his jacket and ripped out the back lining, revealing sticks of dynamite and a roll of detonation cord. He carefully laid the dynamite among the crates. He unraveled the det cord and started to insert the fuses when suddenly . . .

A cigarette lighter flicked from across the room, illuminating the face of Major Smith as he lipped a cigarette from a pack, held it to the flame, took a deep drag, and stepped from the shadows into the glow of the lantern. In his other hand he held a Colt .45 automatic pistol, aimed sure and steady center-mass at the blond saboteur.

The saboteur froze in place. He let out a breath, shook his head, grinned, and said, in the Queen's perfect English, "Scared me for a second there, old chap."

Smith took another drag on the stick, blew a calm stream of smoke, and said nothing.

"You're Smith, right? Major Smith, US Army Intelligence?"

Smith glanced at his watch, said nothing, and took another puff.

"I'm with the Second Fusiliers. Captain Thomas. Wynn Thomas. We've been tracking this cargo since—"

Smith yanked the hammer back, spoke hard, "Let 'em talk long enough and they'll talk themselves into a grave. There is no Second Fusiliers in Britain. What are you? French? Dutch? No, you're not Dutch—they're just not that dumb."

They looked at each other. The jig was up.

"*French?*" the saboteur spat. His accent had changed. It was now Russian. "I am Russian," he said. "And you're not going to fire that pistol in here, not in this powder keg. Even a pacifistic American is not that crazy."

Smith treaded over to the saboteur. Flipped his pistol around, held it out to the saboteur, grip first.

"You're right," he said, holding his free hand up in surrender. "You win. We're pacifists, us Yanks. Every last one of us."

As the saboteur hesitantly started to reach for the gun being offered to him, the tenth of a second of confusion was enough for Smith to suddenly club him across the face with the heavy pistol.

The saboteur went down like a ton of bricks.

Less than an hour later, Smith had the saboteur tied to a railing overlooking the grinding turbines deep down in the hot engine room of the *Lusitania*.

Smith slapped the saboteur. He slowly came to.

"What's your name?" Smith growled.

The saboteur glared at him.

"Boris?"

No response.

"Ivan? I think I'll call you Ivan. Ivan, do you see where you are?"

Ivan looked around—noticed that he was tied with coils and coils of detonation cord, binding his arms, chest, and legs to the steel rail. The sparking turbines were chugging away below. He stood very still.

"Sorry old sport," Smith said. "Had to use det cord because, well, it was available, wasn't it. And you're a pretty big fella, so I had to use a lot."

He retrieved a cigarette, lit it with a wooden match, and casually tossed it on the floor near Ivan's feet.

"Oops," Smith said humorlessly, watching the match flame flicker and then sputter out. "Guess I should be more careful around your flammable wrapping, shouldn't I. Wouldn't want Ivan to go up in smoke now, would we?"

They looked at each other. Ivan's eyes narrowed.

"I've seen that look before," Smith grinned, using his cigarette as a pointer at Ivan. "You're thinking, *This American is crazy*." He tossed his cigarette on the floor, mashed it out angrily, saying, "And you would be right, Ivan. I am very crazy." He grinned.

"I am a Russian!" Ivan blurted. "I will die fighting to protect Mother Russia!"

"Oh, I know you will. Pretty soon. Be patient. I'm not finished with you just yet."

"You Americans hide like frightened little girls, but you sell the Allies whatever they want!" Ivan said and spat on the floor at Smith's feet. "Blood money! But you are not willing to die for your friends. Will your country stand up when Germany invades your shores, bombs your cities, rapes and kills your women and children? Never! Cowards."

Smith glared at him. Took a deep breath . . . let it out slowly, trying to control himself.

He said, "The time for big talk is done. Now, you will tell me who is working with you."

Ivan looked away, lips shut, jaw clenched tight.

"I am assuming you are right handed," Smith said, pulling the box of matches from his pocket.

Ivan looked at him, puzzled.

Smith stepped closer to Ivan. Struck a match. Lit a length of cord that was hanging down twelve inches from Ivan's right hand and that was wrapped around his wrist. The fuse burned fast, quickly encircling Ivan's wrist. Ivan gritted his teeth, but made no sound as his flesh and hair burned.

"Who else is working with you?!"

"*Poshel ty*!" he yelled angrily, his face refusing to display his agony as his hand smoked.

"Who is Poshel Ty!?"

Ivan started to laugh. He said, "Screw you is *poshel ty*! You think Russia is the only one who knows how to get America into this war!?"

A gunshot suddenly rang out—Ivan slammed backward, a bloody hole in his chest.

Smith spun around—saw Cornwell standing a few feet behind him, a smoking Webley .455 pistol in his hand.

Cornwell used the pistol like a pointer, waving it in the direction of Ivan's leg.

"Damn near got you there, old boy."

Smith's eyes followed the direction of the barrel of Cornwell's gun to Ivan's leg. The leg was stretched out toward Smith. Jutting out from the front of his boot was a gleaming, sharp blade.

"Old Russki trick," Cornwell said. "Poison tip, no doubt."

Suddenly, the det cord wrapped around Ivan lit up—flames raced around his body like a sparkler on the Fourth of July, around and around him. Ivan fought against the cords, writhing in agony. His clothes and hair caught fire. He suddenly broke free of his bonds, leapt at Smith—flaming arms stretched out in front of him. Smith stepped back—wrenched his pistol from his pit holster—shot Ivan in the forehead.

Ivan slammed backward over the rail and tumbled down into the churning, grinding turbines.

CHAPTER 16

The Pulse Weapon

The lights in Tesla's lab in Bulkhead 51 began to flicker and dim. Tesla and Li, who were hunkered over the workbench, tinkering with the sonar wave detector test model, looked up at the ceiling lights.

"Curses!" Tesla exclaimed. "Not *now!*"

They watched as the sonar test model began to power down . . . then surged . . .

"No, *no!*"

. . . Then smoked . . . then shorted out . . .

"Li, do something!"

"Like what, Boss!?"

. . . Then sputtered . . . and died.

"Curses on that Thomas Alva Edison! His DC current will be the death of the planet before people catch on to how inferior it is!"

The lights began to flicker back on, illuminating the extent of the ruined experiment.

"Not to worry, Boss. I think I can fix it."

The lab was suddenly thrown into pitch-black darkness.

"I guess I'm the electrical engineer," Tesla said, sparking his arc cigarette lighter. "Looks like it's up to me to fix this. Let's go, Li."

They treaded to the bulkhead door in the dim blue glow of the electric spark and stepped out into the corridor. As they threaded their way down staircases and through narrow corridors, headed toward the engine room and the generators below, they came to a smoke-filled passage with a flashing red warning light.

Tesla pulled a handkerchief from a pocket, covered his mouth and nose, saying to Li, "Stay here. If I'm not back in two minutes, come get me."

"It would be much better for your health to take some fresh air topside," Major Smith's voice suddenly cut through the smoke behind them.

Tesla and Li spun around and saw Smith and Cornwell walking out of the red-hued smoke like wraiths, handkerchiefs held to their faces.

Cornwell said, "Out for a stroll, are you, old chap?"

"So this is what it takes to get you out of your hole, eh, Tesla?" Smith said. "What, homesick for Wardenclyffe and your fireworks?"

"No. What brings me out of my 'hole' as you so crudely put it, is the fact that I need electricity in order to do my work."

"And you think you can fix it, do you?" Smith said. "Just because you're the famous Nikola Tesla?"

"The fact that I am an electrical engineer seems to suddenly escape you, Major Smith. I am losing valuable work time while we stand here chatting. Is there some reason you are fearful of allowing me down to the generator room to see if I may be of assistance?"

"Fearful?" Smith snapped. "I'm not afraid of anyth—"

"Think of electricity as a lion," Li cut in. "It can be dangerous and unruly. And on this boat, Mr. Tesla is the king of all lion tamers. So, if you put your head in the lion's mouth, you better know what you're doing or—" he abruptly slapped his hands together, making Smith flinch—"*crunch!* You'll get your head bitten clean off."

"Why, you little!—"

"Major Smith," Tesla said, stepping between Smith and Li, "What Li is saying is that we simply came to see if we could be of any assistance with the power outage. We depend on a consistent supply of electricity in order to conduct our experiments and construct our prototypes. Otherwise, a full day's work will be lost because of a power outage like this."

Suddenly, the red light stopped flashing and the ceiling lights came on again.

"There," Cornwell said, waving a hand in the direction from which Tesla and Li had come. "Lion tamed. No need to go any farther. You're back in business. Carry on."

"I would feel much better if I knew what caused this problem," Tesla said. "I cannot afford to have it occur again."

"It was the damnedest thing," Smith said, standing in front of Tesla, blocking the passage, arms folded across his chest, "It seems a little blond rat fell into one of the turbine generators."

"Dirty little bugger," Cornwell added. "Burned to a crisp—*fssst*—just like that."

Tesla looked from Cornwell to Smith to Li. He shook his head, turned to go back to the lab, and said to Li, "Let's go, Li. These men seem to be drinking again."

As Tesla and Li made their way toward the Bulkhead 51 lab, crewmen closing doors to smoke-filled corridors rerouted them. Soon, they found themselves lost in a seemingly endless maze of corridors in the bowels of the massive ship.

"Let's get topside and get our bearings," Tesla said.

They headed down the long narrow corridor, but soon reached another dead end. They turned around and stopped to assess where they were.

"Must be a stairway or a ladder or something around here," Li said.

"You lead. I'll follow."

They headed back down the corridor, bypassing several padlocked cargo hold doors.

"This could take forever," Li said. "Has to be a shortcut around here."

They stopped. Li examined the chains on a cargo door wheel. He pulled a length of wire from his belt and began picking the padlock.

"That's not something you learned from me," Tesla quipped.

"No. But handy to know," Li said and grinned.

He had the lock open in seconds. He grabbed the wheel, gave it a spin, and pulled open the heavy steel door. They stepped into the room and made their way through a vast quantity of barrels and crates stacked high and emerged in a wide, open area.

On the floor in the center was a large, canvas-covered crate on a pallet. Just beyond that was a ladder leading up to a ceiling hatch.

"There," Tesla said, pointing. "Up the ladder we go."

As they padded around the large crate, Tesla casually looked down at the exposed wood on the bottom of the pallet. He did a double take. Li's eyes followed Tesla's gaze. Burned into the wood was a single word: *Wardenclyffe*.

In unison, without saying a word, they yanked off the canvas. Li grabbed a wooden slat, pounded it with his fist, loosening it enough to wrench it free. He reached in, ripped the packing straw away, and he and Tesla pressed their faces to the opening.

In the crate was Tesla's oscillating pulse weapon.

"Good God!" Tesla exclaimed. "What the—!"

"Smith!" Li cried out. "I should have known it—never trust a psycho with a uniform and a gun!"

They ripped more boards from the crate. Tesla reached in and opened the breech. The core was gone.

"It's useless," Tesla said. He looked at Li and added, "And thank God for that. Far away, right, Li? You put it far, far away, like I told you? Correct?"

Li gulped and said, "Um, yes, Boss. Farthest place I could think of. At the time."

"Captain Turner must be told about this. Smuggling this aboard the *Lusitania* puts the entire ship in danger."

"Not so fast, gentlemen," came Cornwell's voice.

Tesla and Li spun around. Smith and Cornwell came toward them.

"What the hell!" Tesla snapped. "Is sneaking up on people like this part of your training, or is it just a hobby with you two?"

"We're at war," Cornwell replied. "The entire world is in danger. Not just this ship."

"And it's our job to be one step behind you, Tesla," Smith said. "So you don't get yourself into any trouble."

"Trouble?" Tesla said. "This is stolen property! If anybody is in trouble, it's whoever took it from my lab without my consent."

"Like the colonel said, Mr. Tesla, this is war. All bets are off. Desperate times call for desperate measures."

"But the gun is useless without the core," Tesla said. "It's just a hunk of cold metal."

Smith climbed up on the crate and peered into the empty breech.

He stepped down, faced Tesla, asking in a hard voice, "Where is it?"

"That is none of your concern."

Smith raised a hand to strike Tesla—Li abruptly grabbed his hand by the wrist mid-strike.

Smith shook him off.

Li moved into a self-defense stance.

Cornwell said, "Now, now, Major. We can't have Mr. Tesla all banged up, can we? Two more days, that's all, then it's over."

"I want them both locked up, confined to quarters under guard!" Smith snapped.

"Calm down, Major Smith. We can handle two more days. I'm sure Mr. Tesla will comply. After all, where are they going to go?" He turned to Tesla and said, "And you, sir. Now that you're out of your little cocoon, I'm sure Captain Turner will be delighted to have you back at his table once again, with your military escort, Major Smith, sitting by your side."

"Even if we have to drag you there," Smith said. "And if you decide to tell anyone what you've seen, including Captain Turner—"he put a hand inside his jacket, patted his pistol—"you could find yourself on the wrong end of an unfortunate accident." He looked coldly at Li and added, "The same goes for you. Say a word, and your little girlfriend could suddenly find herself taking a midnight swimming lesson in the Atlantic."

"Now," Cornwell said with a condescending smile and a patronizing pat on Tesla's back, "what say we all freshen up and enjoy a good supper together, ey? This will all be over faster than you can spell *Lusitania*."

CHAPTER 17

Shakedown at Bulkhead 51

Later that evening in the first-class dining room, tables had been moved to the sides of the spacious room, and the elite, the wealthy, and the landed gentry were cutting a rug to the band's rendition of Olive Kline and Reinald Werrenrath's light little love ballad, "Hello Frisco!"

"Hello, Frisco, hello! Hello, New York, hello. I love you only. I've been so lonely.

Tell meee, have youuu been truuue?"

At his table, Captain Turner was hosting Tesla, Vanderbilt, Smith, Cornwell, Frohman, Hubbard, the usual crew.

Tesla, with a dour look on his face, was watching dispassionately as Li and Claire were on the floor, dancing to the tune, gaily mouthing the lyrics to each other. Li's moves weren't all that bad.

"Where'd you learn to dance so well?" Claire asked him as they danced the ragtime.

"I didn't," Li said. "These are just some Shuai jiao moves sped up a little, with some Five Animals of Shaolin mixed in for good taste."

At the captain's table, Vanderbilt called across the table to Tesla, "Nikola, you look like a child sulking on the sidelines of a playground after a bully stole his baseball."

Wouldn't be the first time, Tesla thought morosely and took a sip of whiskey.

Vanderbilt stood, treaded over to Tesla, and pulled a Cuban cigar from a jacket pocket. "You know," he said, unwrapping the cigar, "there is some truth to the old saying 'You need to get out more.'"

"I'm quite busy on a new invention," Tesla replied.

"What sort of invention could be so important that you'd want to hole up in the hot bowels of this steel bucket in the middle of a beautiful trip like this, old boy? Damn well better be something that could end the war."

The party at the table chuckled and clinked glasses.

Tesla pulled out his electrode lighter and lit Vanderbilt's cigar for him. Vanderbilt patted him on the back, thanked him, and strolled to his chair.

The band started into another song and the upbeat mood changed as the crooner at the mic shifted into Morton Harvey's popular protest tune "I Didn't Raise My Boy to Be a Soldier."

" . . . There'd be no war todayyy if mothers all would sayyyy, I didn't raise my boy to be a soldierrrr . . ."

Li and Claire walked back to the table, watching Tesla all the way.

Claire said to Li, "I'm concerned about his health."

They reached the table. Claire sat on one side of Tesla, Li on the other.

Claire leaned to Tesla and said, "Nicky . . . you don't eat, you don't sleep, you just work work work down in your dungeon."

"And I thought he'd just grown tired of the same old faces at the captain's table," Frohman said.

Everyone chuckled. Except Captain Turner. And Smith and Cornwell.

"Maybe he's just doing what I plan to do once we're in German infested waters," Hubbard said.

"What's that?" Frohman said, "hiding under your bed?"

"No. Under yours. It's more heavily fortified," Hubbard quipped.

More chuckling. Even Smith cracked a smile.

Vanderbilt said, "Nikola, tell us about this new invention you said you're working on."

Smith and Cornwell shot Tesla a look at the same time.

Li spoke up before Tesla could respond. "Mr. Tesla's inventions are designed to serve mankind, to help people." Li paused, looked at Smith, and continued, "But there are people who would like to see his creations used for darker purposes."

"Well on that cheerful note," Vanderbilt said, "I guess we all know the saying, 'War is hell.'" He looked at Tesla, adding, "You are constantly involved in wars of sorts, Nikola."

"How's that?" Tesla asked.

"Your own War of Currents, as the newspapers called it, with Tom Edison, as one example. Yet, look who won that one: you got the '93 Worlds Fair contract. Lit up Chicago with AC power like Chinese fireworks. Then Niagara Falls and the world's first hydroelectric power plant. And what about that teleautomaton show you put on at Madison Square Garden in '98, the remote-controlled boat? Brilliant! People thought it was either magic or mental telepathy."

"I heard you did that one with a miniature monkey," Frohman deadpanned.

The group laughed.

Claire said, "He's lost some wars too."

All heads turned to Claire.

She continued. "Mostly because he gets taken advantage of—I suspect because he's more of a lover than a fighter."

"What war did you lose, Mr. Tesla?" Hubbard asked.

"*Wars*," Li said. "Several of them. Fifteen years ago he was awarded patents for his invention that transmitted electrical energy. The following year, Guglielmo Marconi made that world's first transatlantic radio transmission and was granted a patent for it—using the same system Mr. Tesla had already invented."

"There, that proves it," Frohman said. "Anybody who comes up with any revolutionary idea is instantly at war with someone who's out to take him down."

"And like all wars," Smith said, "somebody has to lose."

"As long as they don't do so by cheating," Li said. "Some day I'm going to visit Marconi and ask to see Nikola Tesla's Nobel Prize."

Smith said, "Don't you appreciate irony? Marconi has a wireless radio room named after him on this very ship. The technology you, Mr. Tesla, claim to have invented. That must hurt."

The room went quiet at the cruel shot.

Vanderbilt broke the chill. "All I'm saying is this man, Nikola Tesla, is a fighter, a warrior. You don't accomplish what he has in this world without standing up for what you believe, against all foes, no matter how powerful or intimidating. Right is right!"

The band struck up a waltz.

Claire stood, held out a hand to Tesla. He looked up at her, unsure.

"You wouldn't deny this beautiful young woman the pleasure of a dance, would you?" Captain Turner asked.

Tesla looked pleadingly at Mark Twain, who was sitting there, sipping from a glass of green mint liqueur.

"Oh, go on," Twain said, his eyes twinkling at Tesla. "You're too young to act like such a poop. Go dance with the girl!" He took another sip, grinned, and added, "Or I will, by golly!"

Claire smiled at Tesla and reached out her other hand. Before he could protest, she had grabbed both his hands and was pulling him onto the dance floor.

Tesla was awkward on his feet.

Claire said, "Don't get out much, huh—you do know how to waltz, right?"

"Of course," Tesla replied. "It's just . . . been awhile."

His moves were stiff but the music did its work. Tesla quickly loosened up and began gliding with her. Li smiled as he watched them dance.

Tesla's eyes caught Twain, holding his glass up in salute and grinning widely. "Way to go, my boy!"

Claire said to Tesla, "It's glorious to be alive, isn't it, Nicky?"

Her words were soothing. Soon they were swirling like professionals.

Suddenly, the spell was broken as the band came to an awkward and abrupt stop, and the drummer did a drum roll.

A spotlight was thrown onto Captain Turner, who was standing, with a note in his hand.

"Pardon the interruption, ladies and gentlemen," Turner said. He paused, looked at everyone, and then announced, "By the time we awake tomorrow morning, the *Lusitania* will be in the war zone."

A murmur of concern rumbled through the crowd.

Turner continued. "There is no need for alarm. The might of His Majesty's Royal Navy will accompany us all the way to Liverpool. We couldn't be in better hands."

Tesla, standing there with Claire in his arms, looked over at Smith and Cornwell.

Turner added, "As a final precaution for our safety, we need to eliminate our visibility as much as possible. So, please keep your shades down tight and do not light cigarettes or cigars on deck tonight."

Vanderbilt looked at his barely smoked Cuban cigar and deadpanned, "You see? What did I say?—war is bloody hell."

* * *

A couple hours ahead in the dead of night in the British Parliament war room, Winston Churchill was taking a puff on his own cigar, adding to the musty cloud hanging over him and Kitchener.

Kitchener slammed back a drink and said, "You're not pleased? There are nearly 2,000 people on board the *Lusitania*."

Churchill said, "At least 150 who happen to be Americans."

"I'm talking about British civilians . . . women and children! Not to mention Tesla and America's super weapon."

"Bollocks! The only good that so-called super weapon could do is be on the bottom with as many of those damn Yanks floating around it as possible for all their foot-dragging and fearmongering. Neutrality my ass!" He tossed a paper across the table at Kitchener and added, "Our agent who stopped the Russian spy on the *Lusitania*? Remind me to pin a medal on him. And then have him shot. It could have all been over, with no one to blame but the Tsar!"

Kitchener said, "Looks like it's Britannia all the way from here. *Lusitania* will be in U-boat patrolled waters by sunrise. Shall I proceed with Prime Minister Asquith's request to double the escort?"

Churchill's eyes reflected the red glow of his cigar as his small eyes, buried in the bulk of his heavy face, squinted in thought.

Finally, he said, "You go on. I'll put it in. They'll want confirmation anyway. Good night."

Kitchener left the room. Churchill added more smoke to the cloud floating around him, his mind exploring dark options that could haunt a man for life.

* * *

On the rear deck of the *Lusitania*, as the grand liner headed deeper into the blackness of night, with all shades drawn and lights off, a door opened and Li stepped to the rail. He pulled a sturdy metallic case from beneath his jacket. He opened the case. The dim bluish glow of the core lit his features as he looked at it.

"Sorry, Boss," he muttered to himself. "You said *far, far away* . . . but at the time, the other side of the world seemed pretty far to me."

Li looked at the wake churning rapidly into the distance behind the behemoth ship . . . nothing but black water as far as the eye could see.

He picked up the core, cocked his arm back—and suddenly, Claire said from behind him, "Li? What are you doing out here?"

He quickly brought his arm down, slipped the core into its case, snapped it shut, and turned to see Claire approaching.

"Oh . . . just . . . enjoying the last night of peace and quiet out here at sea."

"What say we enjoy the last night together . . . in your suite?"

He turned. They embraced. Her face was close, her breath warm, her body fit his perfectly.

She said, "I can't promise you too much peace and quiet, though."

Two hours later, Tesla knocked on Li's door.

"Li! Li—wake up!"

The door opened to reveal Li in a state of bleary-eyed bliss. The room looked like it had barely survived a cyclone.

"Li?" Tesla said, his eyes cautiously scanning the room. "Good God man . . . are you all right?"

The bathroom door opened behind Li. Claire stepped out. Tesla's eyes went wide.

Claire said, "Oh, he's better than all right, Nicky. And he's not done yet."

Tesla looked at Li. Li grinned. Tesla looked at Claire. Claire smiled. Her left eyebrow flicked upward.

"If you're thinking about dragging him off, Nicky," Claire said, "you can forget about it."

Tesla looked back at Li and stammered, "L-Li I need you—now! We need to destroy the, the, you know—the . . . *thing*."

Li sobered up instantly. He jabbed a finger at Claire and told her, “Get dressed and stay here. Lock the door behind us when we leave and open it to no one.”

“Wha?—Li, I'm a part of this, whether you boys like it or not! Especially in matters of science!” She stopped talking and watched him stumble into his trousers; a smile melting over her face, she added sensuously, “And in matters of . . . mmmm . . . you know.”

“Look,” Tesla cut in, “there are forces at work here that could cause you great harm, Ms. LeFleur, and—”

“Oh, I'm suddenly Ms. LeFleur when I'm in—”

“This is no time for joking!” Tesla snapped.

Claire shut up. Li finished dressing.

Tesla said, “I'm sorry, but I cannot allow you to be put in harm's way, Claire.”

“Are you forgetting why I'm here in the first place,” Claire said softly.

Tesla took a breath and then said, “I apologize, Doctor. Of course I know. But . . . this is too dangerous for a woman. I . . . I don't want you hurt.”

Claire grabbed her dress, flung it over her head, and replied, “It could be that I'm a dangerous woman, Dr. Tesla. It could be that you would need a dangerous woman like me with you. I'm coming.”

Li looked at Tesla, saying, “She does have her good points, Boss.”

They studied each other for a moment. Tesla pulled out his pocket watch, looked at it . . . paused in confusion . . . and tapped it, muttering, “Damn thing's been acting up lately.” He looked at them and said, “Two minutes. You have exactly two minutes. Then I leave. With or without you.”

He closed the door as Claire continued getting dressed.

Ten minutes later, in the lower deck corridors and bulkheads, Tesla, Li, and Claire stealthily made their way toward the hold containing the pulse weapon. They halted before turning down the corridor to the hold. Tesla peeked around the corner. The cargo hold was unguarded. He glanced back at them, an odd look on his face.

"Something's wrong," he whispered.

He motioned them forward. They reached the cargo hold: the door was wide open and there were fresh scrape marks on the steel frame. They peered inside. Cargo obscured their view. Tesla stepped in. They wound their way through the crates and stacks of steel drums.

Tesla said, "I've got a bad feeling about this."

Claire said, "About what? What exactly are we looking for?"

Tesla shot her a look, put his finger to his lips, and led them forward toward the crate. They stopped. In front of them lay the splintered remnants of the crate that had held the pulse weapon only last night.

"*No!*" Tesla said in a hard whisper.

"They've moved it!" Li said.

"Will somebody please tell me what *it* is?" Claire said too loudly.

"Shut up!" Tesla barked.

She shut up.

And Cornwell said, "Thank you."

Tesla, Li, and Claire spun around to see Cornwell. Smith was at his side with his Colt .45 automatic in his fist aimed in a very deadly direction.

Smith said to Cornwell out the side of his mouth, "Told you they'd come here."

"Where is it?!" Tesla demanded.

"Safely put away. As I'm afraid you're about to be, as well."

Cornwell pulled his Webley from its holster and used it to motion them toward the door. They all moved in that direction.

Smith jammed his gun into Claire's back.

Li started to react.

Smith pulled back the hammer on the big gun and growled, "Don't get any ideas, Chinaman. Or I'll be happy to shut her up for good."

Smith and Cornwell herded them out of the hold, through the dim corridors. They entered Tesla's lab. Cornwell closed the door and spun the wheel locked.

Smith kicked Li behind the knees, trying to force him to the ground. Li easily caught his balance, spinning to face Smith, where he got a close-up view of the big bore of Smith's Colt .45. He stopped, eye to eye with Smith.

"Give me a reason, Chinaman."

Li remained motionless, his dark, expressionless eyes boring into Smith.

Tesla said, "That weapon won't work without me and Li."

Smith backed off, easing the hammer down on the gun. But he kept it aimed at his captives.

Cornwell addressed Tesla. "I know it's hard for you to see it, Dr. Tesla, but this is for the good of humanity. We're on the same side."

Smith said, "The door will be locked from the outside and a guard will be posted until we dock in Liverpool. Until then, you are going to build a new firing core for that thing."

Tesla scoffed and said to Cornwell, "There never was a British sonar project, was there, Colonel?"

"No. There never was. But I'm sure your work here has not been in vain. Knowing you, you're probably quite close to another breakthrough. Like it or not . . . you might just be responsible for winning this war for us, Nikola Tesla."

Smith added with a sneer, "Yeah. Too bad you won't live to get that Nobel Prize."

Smith and Cornwell exited, slamming and locking the steel bulkhead door as they left.

As they walked down the corridor, Smith said to Cornwell, "You take first watch. I'm going to make sure that weapon is secure. I want no more surprises."

Cornwell nodded and watched Smith disappear down the hallway.

* * *

In Tesla's lab, Li and Tesla heaved with all their strength against the wheel, trying to open it. The wheel wouldn't budge.

Claire said, "How long will it take you to build a new core?"

"Forever," Tesla said. "Because even if I did have the proper tools and materials, I'd never do it. Not for those two psychotic warmongers."

"We should be able to buy time, as long as they think they need us," Li said.

"What exactly is this core?"

"It powers the pulse weapon, which can't be fired without it. Li removed it in New York, before the weapon was stolen, thank God." He looked at Li, adding, "Right, Li? You removed it, right?"

Li wagged his head noncommittally.

Tesla lowered his chin, looked at him, and enunciated each word: "Li. Tell me you did destroy that core, like I instructed you to before we left."

Li continued to waffle. "Boss we talked about not destroying it, but . . ."

"All right then, just reassure me that you put it somewhere in a safe place." Tesla interrupted.

Li cleared his throat and said in a meek voice, "Boss? Remember when you said 'far, far away'?"

"Yes. Keep talking."

"Well . . . at the time . . . England seemed about as far away as—"

"It's *here?!* You brought the core aboard so you could take it to England!?"

Li shrugged.

"Where!?"

"It's secure, Boss. Locked in its lead-lined case."

"*Where?*"

"In my room. Under my bed."

"Under. Your. Bed?! Why not just put it in a shoebox on the captain's table in the middle of dinner! You think those two psychotics are not tearing our rooms to shreds right this minute, searching for it?!"

"Sorry, Boss."

"How much time do we have?"

Tesla pulled out his pocket watch to look. Suddenly he held it closer to his face and shook it.

"Good God," he said. "The second hand is going counterclockwise! It's the core, causing an electro-gravitational resonance!

That's why my watch has been malfunctioning. Li, show me your timepiece."

Li fished his watch from his pocket, holding it up for them to look at. The second hand on Li's watch was also going counterclockwise.

"That explains everything! How could I miss it!"

Claire said, "I take it this core thing is quite dangerous?"

"Deadly," Tesla replied.

"How deadly?"

Li said, "It could sink this entire ship in minutes."

Claire stated calmly, "Well then . . . I guess it's up to us to do something about it."

She suddenly ran to the door as if her hair were on fire and began frantically pounding on it like a madwoman, shrieking, "HELP! Open the door! We have a medical emergency in here! Help!"

Tesla said calmly, "Claire . . . Claire. That will accomplish nothing. Save your breath."

She stopped pounding and said, "Well . . . it was worth a try."

Suddenly, the wheel on the door began spinning. The lock disengaged. The door squeaked open—two men with weapons rushed in—one butted Li in the face with a gunstock—the other shoved Tesla to the floor, grabbed Claire, and dragged her out the door. All in under five seconds.

The door slammed shut and the wheel was spun hard by the time Tesla and Li leaped up from the floor and rushed at it.

Momentarily dazed, they looked at each other.

"Who else knows where it's hidden?" Tesla asked.

"Just us, Boss. Well . . . except her, too, now."

"They couldn't have heard us through the door. They have no reason to believe it's on board, and no reason to believe she knows anything about it. She should be all right. They've taken her as insurance, that's all."

Tesla examined the rivets lining the heavy door, tried the wheel, turned to the workbench, and looked through the tools and materials.

"Got a plan, Boss?"

"Not yet. But problems are merely solutions waiting to be discovered."

His eyes fell on the original, old version of the sound oscillator, sitting under the workbench.

Tesla grabbed the device. Within minutes, they had it attached to the bulkhead door. Li ran a power cable to a battery while Tesla adjusted the power regulator on the device.

"Fifty percent?" Tesla asked Li. "Thirty?"

"Your call, Boss. We'll either end up in the corridor . . . or on the other side of the ship—in a real jiffy."

"Forty should be about right."

Li said, "Let's go with 33 percent."

Li turned the heavy steel lab table on its side. He and Tesla ducked behind it. Li held the wire above the Edison battery terminal.

Tesla said, "Never thought I'd be thanking Edison for anything."

"If it works, Boss, if it works."

"True. And even then, he's still a jackass."

Tesla nodded and gave Li a thumbs-up.

"Fire in the hole!" Li said.

He put the wire to the terminal. It sparked. The oscillator hummed to life. The door began to vibrate.

In the corridor outside the lab door, the guard sensed the door vibrating. He looked at it. He bashed on it with the butt of his machine gun.

"You in there!" he yelled. "Back away from the door!"

The vibrating increased. His bravado began to melt as the floor began to vibrate.

Inside the lab, the humming was eardrum shattering. Tesla and Li, palms tight over their ears, watched as the door vibrated, rivets came loose, and the locking wheel began to slowly turn.

Out in the hallway, the guard grabbed the spinning wheel as it sped up—his grip was broken—his arm cracked by the force of the increasing rotation. His gun clattered to the ground. He grabbed his arm, backed away, eyes wide in fear. The hum increased to a deafening pitch—rivets began blasting off the steel door and peppering the corridor like machine gun fire. The guard slid down the wall and plopped to the floor, dead.

In the lab, Tesla motioned at Li. "Shut it down! Shut it down!"

Li ripped the wire lead from the battery. The vibrating and humming wound down. Tesla and Li leapt over the table and rushed out the door.

Li looked around but saw nobody.

"All clear!" he said.

Tesla looked at the blood pooling around the dead guard whose face was obscured by the edge of the door.

Li leaned down, moved the guard's head for a clear look, put a finger on his carotid artery.

Li turned to Tesla, shook his head, and said, "Dead."

"Then that's on Smith," Tesla said, his voice hard. "Li, we must destroy that pulse weapon."

Li said, "And find Claire. What's our plan, Boss?"

Tesla pointed at the guard's gun and said, "Grab that."

Li pulled the guard's machine gun from under his body and started to rack the bolt—but the gun instantly fell to pieces in his hands.

Li looked from the pile of metal to Tesla, asking, "What's our new plan, Boss?"

Tesla looked at the gun parts scattered across the floor and then at the oscillator on the fallen door.

"Go grab the battery. I'll get the oscillator."

Tesla untangled the oscillator from the door. Li followed the long wires back to the battery in the lab. One wire was dangling free, the other still connected to the terminal. He rolled the loose wire around his hand and lugged the battery to the door next to Tesla.

Tesla raised his watch toward the left, held it for a moment, watching the second hand: the hand moved clockwise. He moved it to the right: the hand slowed . . . stopped . . . began going counterclockwise.

He pointed right and said, "This way!"

Li doubled his grip on the battery. They headed down the hallway, making their way up to their suites separated by a ten-foot length of electrical wire connected to the oscillator and a battery terminal.

They entered Li's room. It was ransacked—looking even worse than after his earlier encounter with Claire.

Li searched under his bed, pulled out the core case, and opened it. It was empty.

Li looked up at Tesla and exclaimed, "They took it!"

Tesla looked at his watch, saw the second hand ticking counterclockwise. He closed the core case and looked at his watch again. The hand slowed . . . stopped . . . reversed to clockwise.

"Good. We have a detector of sorts," he said.

Li looked at Tesla fearfully and responded, "But Claire's in big trouble."

"Don't assume they forced her to tell them where it was, Li. I mean . . . you hid it *under the bed*. May as well have put a sign on your front door."

"Okay, I get your point, bad hiding job. But she's still missing, Boss! No telling what they're doing to her."

"True," Tesla said. He grabbed the oscillator. "Stay close—and don't let that wire touch the terminal. Let's go!"

Li grabbed the battery, a worried look on his face.

They ran.

CHAPTER 18

The Schwieger Approach

The next day, May 7, 1915, was a gray day with poor visibility. At the lifeboat stations, the crew was engaged in the vigorous hustle and bustle of preparing the lifeboats. Passengers watched in idle curiosity as stewards, deckhands, and crewmembers worked together, efficiently swinging the lifeboat davits out.

Elbert Hubbard, elegantly attired and wearing a thick wool jacket, was strolling arm in arm with his wife Alice, a matronly woman in a long, heavy, ornately decorated dress.

"Elbert, what do you suppose they're doing? We're nowhere near port just yet, are we?"

"Not really, no, dear."

Just then, the crew started to distribute life jackets to the passengers. The passengers' curiosity began to fade to puzzlement.

A steward approached the Hubbards with life jackets.

Hubbard asked, "Young man, why do we need these?"

"Only a precaution, sir."

"Precaution?" Mrs. Hubbard asked. "Against what?"

"Yes, against what?" Mr. Hubbard repeated. "What do we have to fear that we need life jackets, young man, for heaven's sake?"

"Nothing to be alarmed about, sir and madam. Standard procedure," the steward replied. He smiled, pointed ahead to the left, and added in a friendly, unconcerned tone, "Pretty soon, if you look on the port side, to the left up there, you'll be able to see Old Head of Kinsale. Not ten miles away. Ireland. We'll be arriving soon."

Hubbard said, "Are we in danger?"

"No, no—not at all sir."

He held out the life jackets.

Hubbard waved him off, saying, "Then give us a holler if you find we *are* in danger." He looked at his wife and chuckled. "Unless it's during lunch, when I plan on having shellfish, in which case I might be in danger."

"Oh Elbert."

Hubbard leaned to the steward and said under his breath, "But use discretion, my wife loves her desserts."

The steward smiled politely, held out the life jackets again, saying, "Take them anyway, please. You don't have to wear them. Just keep them handy."

Just then, Vanderbilt brushed by them and leapt up the steps to the navigating bridge by twos.

On the bridge, the quartermaster, a burly man with a face like the surface of the moon, stepped in front of Vanderbilt, holding up a thick hand.

“Sir—you are not allowed on the navigating bridge!”

Vanderbilt plowed past him and burst through the door of the wheelhouse.

In the wheelhouse, Captain Turner and the executive officer were peering intently out the window at the gray ocean spread out before them when Vanderbilt burst in, followed by the quartermaster.

Turner spun around.

Vanderbilt stopped in front of him and said, his breath heaving, “Captain Turner, am I or am I not correct in my understanding that we have in fact entered hostile waters?!”

“Sorry, sir,” the quartermaster said to Turner. “He wouldn’t take no for an answer.”

Turner addressed Vanderbilt calmly. “These are merely precautions, Mr. Vanderbilt. The lifeboats are swung out at the ready, lookouts are at their posts, standard procedure during wartime, that’s all. No further precautions are necessary.”

“That was not my question, Captain. And I might find those assurances more comforting if the Royal Navy escort you promised us was sailing alongside. It is May 7, sir. We are scheduled to arrive today. I see no escort outside and we are approaching Ireland. So, with no escorts and entering enemy infested waters, why does it feel as if we’re slowing down?!”

“Mr. Vanderbilt, this is not your ship, and Cunard Line procedures are not your concern.”

“Answer me! You read the warning sign on the dock in New York City—the Germans have stated—practically *promised*—they will sink any vessel they deem to be bringing aid of any sort to their enemies. Indeed, the Kaiser’s fleet has been doing just that—sinking hundreds of boats, of all kinds!”

"Calm down, Mr. Vanderbilt! You are interfering with the operation of my ship!"

"I have a right to know!"

Turner addressed the quartermaster tersely, "Escort Mr. Vanderbilt from my bridge immediately."

The quartermaster stepped over to Vanderbilt and took him by the elbow.

Vanderbilt shook him off, pulled out a checkbook and a pen, and said to Captain Turner, "I've been on the aft deck. Tell me, Captain Turner, what will it cost to fire up the fourth boiler and engage the remaining engine? Name your price. I'll write you a check this instant. I'll even make it out to you personally."

"Another word and I will have you placed under arrest and locked in the brig!"

"This isn't my first rodeo!" He pocketed the checkbook and pen, held his wrists together, and barked, "Lock me up and throw away the key, if you like! My attorneys will have me out by the time we reach port—if we're lucky enough to reach port at all! You're practically advertising our presence here! If you refuse to go full speed, at least start zigzagging, man! That's standard operating procedure in enemy waters!"

"Mr. Alfred Vanderbilt! You may be the richest man in America, but on this ship there is only one captain! And that is *me!* Now, you are testing my patience! Visibility is not conducive to putting on another engine! Zigzagging wastes time and it wastes fuel! I have taken all prudent precautions. The watertight doors are secured. We have posted double lookouts. A blackout has been in effect the past two nights. Lifeboats are swung out on their davits and can be launched in minutes if needed. Do you understand?!"

The two men glared at each other.

The quartermaster stood at the ready for orders.

The executive officer kept vigilant watch forward.

Vanderbilt lowered his hands and looked at the floor, clenching his jaw. "Apologies," he mumbled.

"Accepted."

The captain let out a breath. He added in a calmer voice, "Alfred, the *Lusitania* has received the all-clear call. The Admiralty itself declared our route free of U-boats and recommended we proceed with caution and due vigilance, but not with alarm." He paused and peered out at the ocean for a moment. Then he added conciliatorily, "The fog has lifted. We planned to increase speed to as much as eighteen knots now anyway."

Vanderbilt looked at Turner but said nothing.

The captain continued, in the softer tone of a caring father to a chastised son. "Look, son . . . do you know more than the Admiralty? Do you have, in your vast resources, anything even approaching the intelligence network that Great Britain possesses?"

They looked at each other for a long beat, each man sizing up the other.

Vanderbilt broke the silence. "It doesn't take vast intelligence resources to sense when something feels . . . horribly wrong."

He turned and strode out of the wheelhouse.

The captain and his officers exchanged looks.

Turner said to his executive officer, "Increase speed to eighteen knots and hold."

"Aye, Captain."

* * *

In the lower deck corridors and bulkheads, Tesla and Li were hunting for the core. Tesla glanced at his watch: the second hand was stuttering backward. They continued apace, Tesla leading the way through the maze of corridors, down a narrow stairway, to the lower decks.

They stepped through a bulkhead door and entered the generator room. Arcs of white light strobbed across the massive engines. Tesla stopped and peered around the huge room. They were separated from the whirling turbines below by the railing from which the Russian saboteur had flown to meet his fate earlier, unbeknownst to them. Pieces of charred fabric embedded with dark chunks of what looked like charcoal were burned into the rail.

Tesla examined the fabric and sniffed the burned sections of railing.

"Steak."

"What?" Li asked.

"Smells like New York strip steak," Tesla said, wrinkling his nose. "Barbequed."

"Must have been one bigass rat," Li said.

"Hmmm . . . big enough to wear human clothes, too."

They continued toward the other end. The second hand on Tesla's watch jumped erratically. They opened a bulkhead door, entering engine room number one. The second hand ticked counterclockwise. They follow it, treading past sweaty fire stokers who were feeding coal into the flames beneath the boiler.

Tesla and Li made their way deeper into the hot, smoky, coal-dust-filled engine room, their shapes becoming barely visible as they pressed onward.

* * *

Meanwhile, off the Irish coast, Captain Walther Schwieger was scanning the horizon from the open hatch of the semi-submerged *U-20* with his binoculars, when he suddenly spotted a plume of black smoke rising on the horizon.

He lowered his glasses, looked at his watch and brought the binoculars back to his eyes. He panned quickly to the Irish coast, then to the growing funnel of smoke in the distance.

He leaned down into the sub, yelling, "Diving stations! Periscope depth!"

He climbed down the ladder into the *U-20*. The hatch closed. The wheel spun hard and tight.

Within seconds, the sleek, steel shark slipped silently beneath the waves.

CHAPTER 19

The Real Rat

As Tesla and Li walked cautiously down a corridor in a forward cargo hold, they reached a junction. Tesla stopped and waved the watch in the direction of the left junction. The hand fluttered. He waved it toward the right junction. The second hand began spinning backward. He looked down the right hallway. It led to a large cargo hold door. He motioned Li.

"This way."

Tesla led Li down the corridor. Li occasionally glanced behind them to make sure they weren't being followed. Tesla glanced ahead periodically, his eyes glued to the counterclockwise spinning of the second hand as it began wildly increasing. He looked up as they walked—and saw, standing in front of him, a vaguely familiar man with a black eye, holding a machine gun. Aimed at them.

Tesla abruptly stopped—Li ran into him.

"Whoa, Boss. Warn me befo—"

Li stopped mid-sentence as he saw the armed man in front of them.

The man nodded at the oscillator and battery, leveled his weapon at them, and took a step back.

"*Vas is das*? (What is that?) Who are you? Ver is Hans?"

Tesla lowered the oscillator and signaled Li to put the battery down.

Li stared blankly at the man . . . and moved the wire in his hand a half-inch from the battery terminal.

The man's face tightened. He pointed his gun at Li, racking the bolt back on the machine gun.

"*Vas is das*!?" (What is that?)

Li nodded at the man's gun, shook his head 'no,' and moved the wire a quarter of an inch from the terminal.

Tesla's mouth opened. He forced a smile at the gunman, saying to Li through gritted teeth, "What are you doing, Li?"

The gunman aimed directly at Li.

Li shook his head again, raised his eyebrows, waved the wire an eighth of an inch from the terminal, nodded at the guy's eye, and said, "Where'd you get the shiner?"

Tesla looked at Li, his eyes wide, mouth slightly agape.

Nobody breathed. They looked at each other across six feet of tense, electric air.

Li nodded his chin at the cargo hold door, moved the wire a fraction closer to the terminal, and said in perfect German, "*Öffnen die tür*." (Open the door.)

The gunman relaxed his finger from the trigger, lowered the barrel, raised a hand, nodded, said soothingly, "*Ja, jaa*," and slapped his palm twice on the door behind him.

They heard a metallic clanking, the wheel on the door started spinning, and the door swung slowly open. There, past the gunman, inside the hold, surrounded by crates, rested the pulse weapon, sitting on its tripod, facing the closed, opposite, exterior access cargo hold door.

Tesla smiled. Li kept the gunman at bay with the wire. Tesla stepped past them, entered the hold, and moved toward the pulse weapon. As he rounded the last crate, he abruptly stopped. Standing in front of him was Major Smith with his arms folded across his chest. Standing next to him was Cornwell who had a pinched look on his face and hands behind his back in typical taciturn British fashion.

"Gentlemen," Smith said. "Welcome. I've been expecting you."

He motioned for the gunman to stand next to him. The gunman moved around them and took a position beside Smith, facing Tesla and Li.

Two other armed, vaguely familiar men appeared from inside the hold and took positions between crates on either side of Tesla and Li.

Li raised the battery for them all to see—indicating the wire and terminal, his face a stone mask.

The first gunman said to Smith in German, "*Sie haben eine bombe*!" (They have a bomb!)

Smith waved him off, responded casually, "*Eh. Anscheinend ja*." (Eh. Apparently so.)

Tesla and Li were dumbstruck.

"You look surprised to see me, gentlemen," Smith said.

He looked from Tesla, to the oscillator he was holding, and to the battery and wire in Li's hands.

"Which is it, then," Li spat. "Spy all along, or paid traitor?"

"Deep cover spy for my homeland. I've actually been training for a moment like this for years."

Li moved the wire toward the battery contact.

Smith pulled a large, odd-looking pistol from his belt, chambered a round, saying, "C96 Mauser broomhandle. Much more efficient than that heavier new army Colt the Americans use." He waved the barrel at the battery in Li's hand and added, "Go ahead, Chinaman—don't let me stop you. Fire that baby up. Right here. Right now. You'll get rid of the super weapon, destroy this entire ship, and kill everyone on board, all in mere seconds."

They looked at each other. Nobody spoke. Li thought through his options. There were none.

Smith spoke. "We have no time for your little game, Li Yín Huǒ. The only reason I'm letting you live right now is because you have work to do." He gestured at the oscillator and battery and a nearby crate, saying, "Disconnect the other wire from the terminal and put them down here."

Tesla and Li did as they were told.

Smith turned to the first gunman and asked in German, "Where is Hans?"

"I don't know," the gunman answered. "He wasn't with them."

Smith looked at Tesla. "Where is the man who was guarding your lab?"

"Something not dissimilar to whatever happened to the big fried rat in the generator room." Tesla replied.

"He had a riveting experience," Li said. "Now, where's Claire?!"

Smith raked his pistol across Li's face—knocking him out cold.

"One can never give a fighter like that too much of a warning," Smith said. He turned to Tesla. "I asked you a question."

Tesla ignored him and faced Cornwell who was standing there, hands still behind his back, watching the action in silence.

"I am shocked and saddened that you stand there silently condoning this activity, Colonel Cornwell."

"Not as surprised as I was to find out this man's real name is Herr Schmitt," Cornwell said, motioning at Smith with his chin. "He's a bloody Hun spy—him and his four saboteurs!"

Cornwell charged at Smith—Smith easily sidestepped him—Cornwell stumbled, revealing that his hands were tied behind him.

Smith pushed Cornwell down onto a crate and barked, "Sit down and shut up."

Tesla looked at the three gunmen, saying, "I thought I recognized you fellows. You're the Germans the Irish detective discovered early on." He addressed Smith: "Good ploy, batting them about like you did when they were caught. Nobody suspected a thing."

"Now, what did you do to Hans?" Smith said.

"Hans?" Tesla said. "Ah, yes, him—the guard at my lab . . . I'm afraid you're down to three saboteurs now."

"Plus a crew of twenty-four under the command of U-boat Kapitänleutnant Walther Schwieger, waiting just beyond that door."

Smith jabbed a thumb behind him at the exterior access door.

All heads turned as they heard the cargo door grinding open, revealing the choppy ocean outside.

* * *

Aboard the *U-20*, a beehive of activity ensued as the crew took up battle stations. Captain Schwieger was manning the periscope as Torpedo Officer Raimund Wiesbach thumbed through an edition of *Jane's All the Worlds Fighting Ships*, looking at descriptions, drawings, and black-and-white photos of various oceangoing vessels.

"She has four funnels," Schwieger was saying as he described what was in his scope. "A schooner rig . . . upward of, say . . . 30,000 tons . . . no sign of escort."

Wiesbach found an illustration, jabbed a finger at it, and said, "There. She's either the *Lusitania* or the *Mauretania*."

"Have a look," Schwieger said, stepping away from the periscope.

Schwieger took the book from Wiesbach. Wiesbach took the scope.

"Her funnels are blackened," Wiesbach said. "Definitely a passenger ship. Making about . . . eighteen knots."

Schwieger took the periscope, peered through at the ship again, and said under his breath, "That's her. Good work, Herr Schmitt. Very good work."

"Time?" he said to Wiesbach.

"13:25, mein Captain."

"Boarding party ready?"

"Standing by, sir."

"Set intercept course. Maintain speed, nine knots. Remain at depth, eleven meters."

"Aye, Captain."

"How is our fuel?"

"Low, Captain."

"Then we need to make this count, don't we, Mr. Wiesbach."

CHAPTER 20

Pull the Trigger

The former Major Smith—also known as the German traitor Herr Schmitt—was bracing himself with one hand on the open exterior door of the *Lusitania*'s cargo hold. His other hand held a pair of binoculars to his eyes as he scanned the ocean.

Tesla was sitting on the floor of the hold with Li's head on his lap. Li, still passed out, had a nasty purple bruise across his left cheek.

Cornwell was tied up, sullenly staring at the steel bulkhead wall. The three guards were stationed strategically around room. No escape was possible.

Smith turned from the view, padded over to the pulse gun, and rubbed a hand along its barrel admiringly.

“Mr. Tesla,” he said. “On behalf of Germany, I want to thank you for this truly magnificent weapon. You will now show me exactly how to operate it, and—in the event we are fortunate enough to be joined by a British Royal Navy escort—tell me precisely how much damage it is capable of doing to an enemy combatant. Now, tell me!”

Tesla’s eye’s flicked in the direction of the familiar voice: “Ha, ha!” Twain chuckled as he leaned against the bulkhead wall. “This guy is a real piece of work, isn’t he?” He looked Tesla in the eyes and added, “A new test for you, my boy. It’s going to be up to you to figure out how to get you and Li out of this one.”

Tesla looked at Schmitt, saying, “You have the weapon and the core. You figure it out.”

“Oh we will, we will. I am particularly looking forward to delivering it personally to Kaiser Wilhelm, with my hand on the trigger, demonstrating that with this super weapon, Germany will rule the world.”

“Or die trying.” Tesla shot back.

“Big talk for a skinny man.” Chirped Schmitt.

Tesla said nothing. He picked up a small bolt from the floor and distractedly twiddled it in his hand while Smith rambled on.

“Nicky, Nicky, Nicky. Make no mistake: you will be standing by my side when I unleash this thing. I so hoped you would be there of your own volition and not wearing chains. America has more or less rejected you as a great man of science, you know. But Europe has always been your home, your friend.”

Tesla said nothing.

Li began to wake up. He opened an eye, groaned, and held a hand to his bruised face.

“Are you all right?” Tesla asked him.

Tesla helped Li to his feet.

The first gunman looked at Li and grinned; using his machine gun to point toward Li's bruised face, he said in choppy English, "Ver did you gettin ze shiner, Chinaman?"

The other two guards laughed.

"From your boss," Li said. "Same as you."

The other two guards laughed even harder. The first gunman threw an angry look at them.

Smith looked at Li and said to Tesla, "I'm afraid your little coolie assistant boy there won't be so lucky as to be joining us in the motherland."

"What have you done with Claire?!" Li cried out.

"Oh . . . she'll be around. She's enjoying a cigarette after our little intermission a few minutes ago."

"What do you mean?! If you've hurt her, so help me—!"

"Ah . . . I rather like that puppy love stuff," Smith said, retrieving a pack of cigarettes from his pocket. He lit the cigarette, blew smoke in Li's direction, and said, "You like that forbidden love with white women, do you, Mr. Li? The women you shouldn't have, but can't help yourself from taking anyway? You know, that lack of discipline will be your undoing someday."

He turned to Tesla, pointed his cigarette at him, and chided, "As for you, Mr. Nikola Tesla, I believe this yellow fellow here is the chink in your armor."

The gunmen laughed.

Smith continued. "It'll do you no good to refuse to help me, Nikola. If you won't, then I do have ways of convincing your assistant to help me. But he may not survive my persuasive techniques."

Just then, the interior cargo hold door opened, and Claire stepped in, tucking her blouse into her skirt. Li's face immediately lit up . . . Until he looked from her, closing the door, to the placid guards who were paying her no attention.

Tesla got it instantly, shook his head sadly, muttering, "Oh no, *nooo*."

Li's face was a mask of confusion, while he fought the obvious, refusing to believe what logic was trying to tell him. He looked from her, to Smith, and back to her.

He addressed Smith hesitatingly. "If you have hurt her in any way, I . . ."

"Oh, I have hurt her, in every way."

Li lunged forward.

"Li—*no!*" Tesla yelled.

Smith aimed the Mauser at Li's head—Li stopped just short of an arm's length from the gun, with his eyes ablaze and breath blasting from his mouth.

Li glared.

Smith smiled, pleasantly. He said, "Did you know that on full auto, this little beauty doesn't only shoot holes, it slices like a surgeon's scalpel?" He playfully aimed the gun at Li's crotch, adding, "Care to lose the family jewels?"

The gunmen chuckled.

Li's eyes were wild, darting around the room for options.

Claire moved next to Smith, reached up, put her hand gently on his gun, and pressed it slowly downward.

She looked at Li and said, "My dearest Li, will you please show me how to operate the weapon? We've shared everything else, and not just once. Why not this too?"

She held up the core.

Li stood there, uncomprehendingly, shattered, heartbroken, and ruined, with his mouth open and his mind reeling.

"No," Tesla stated firmly. "You've done enough damage to him. Leave him out of this. I'll do it."

He treaded to Cornwell and asked, "Have you any cigarettes?"

Cornwell nodded, indicating his jacket pocket. Tesla started to reach in—all three gunmen immediately racked and raised their weapons at him. He gingerly retrieved the cigarettes and held the pack up with two fingers, showing them that was all he had.

Smith nodded them back.

Tesla lipped a cigarette, shook a second one from the pack, and held it up to Cornwell's mouth. Cornwell took it with mumbled thanks.

As Tesla fished his cigarette lighter from his pocket, he said, "When you're defeated, you're defeated—and I'm no stranger to defeat. George Westinghouse used me to help him stave off bankruptcy in '97. Got my patents for a song."

He lit his cigarette, continued his discourse. "J.P. Morgan—whew. Dropped me like a rock in a well in 1904."

He blew a stream of smoke, raised the lighter to Cornwell's cigarette, and continued, "Marconi. There was a loser—ripped me off cold. And got clean away with it."

Cornwell took a grateful drag and nodded thanks.

"Then there was Thomas Alva Edison. What a gasbag. Hosed me good, didn't he. But I have learned to take it all with dignity and with strength—a trait I received from my dear mother Đuka Tesla."

He wagged his cigarette lighter at Cornwell and added, "I guess it's safe to say now, Colonel Cornwell, that you, sir, have turned out to be one of the good guys."

He patted Cornwell on the back . . . and surreptitiously dropped his lighter into Cornwell's tied hands.

"Enough with your *poor me* sad history tea talk!" Smith bellowed. He stepped to Tesla, holding out his hand. "I'll take that lighter. It'll make a nice little gift to the Kaiser."

Tesla faced the open bay, hurled the bolt he had picked up earlier out into the water, and said, "Then go fetch it."

Smith watched the splash outside the cargo door, then turned and glared at Tesla.

Tesla said, "You've got the super weapon, Smith. Or Schmitt. Or whatever your real name is. You're going to have to rule the world without my cigarette lighter."

Schmitt turned, pressed the Mauser's barrel to Li's temple, and looked Tesla in the eye, saying in a low and even voice, "His life is in your hands."

He thumbed back the hammer.

"All right, all right," Tesla said in a weary voice, raising his hands. "You win. Give me the core. Let's get this over with."

Schmitt stood back and motioned to Claire. She stepped over to Tesla, holding out the core—but Schmitt suddenly grabbed it from her hand and moved his gun to Tesla's temple.

"Get that breech opened," he ordered Tesla.

Tesla moved to the pulse weapon and opened the breech. He held his hand out to Schmitt for the core.

"I'll load it," Schmitt said. "Show me. I want to know everything about this thing—how to sight it, fire it, unload it. Then we'll get it ready to transport to the homeland."

"And just how do you plan to do that, if I may ask?" Tesla asked, waving a hand toward the open hull door and to the big, gray ocean outside.

"Since you ask so politely, it's really quite simple. When I signal our U-boat—which is lurking right out there, somewhere close—the captain will put a torpedo in *Lusitania*'s starboard side. In the two hours of mayhem while she sinks to the bottom of the ocean, a boarding party will secure the weapon to the deck of the submarine. And we'll be off."

Li said, "And you're telling us this because you plan to kill us."

"Oh no no no. I'm not *barbaric*, for goodness' sake. I'm only going to kill *you*. Nicky here and your lovely Miss Claire will be accompanying me to Germany, where we will live happily ever after."

He scanned the ocean for a moment, then wagged his gun at Tesla and barked, "Now get back to work!"

Tesla pulled a handkerchief from his pocket and began cleaning the core contacts in the breech.

Schmitt added, "Chop-chop! We're on a schedule. They'll be here any minute."

"Not if First Lord of the Admiralty Winston Churchill has anything to do with it," Cornwell said defiantly.

"Churchill? He'll be the first to sign the surrender treaty when he witnesses the power of Germany's new super weapon. I may even let you pick the first target, Colonel. Cruiser? Destroyer? Battleship?"

* * *

At Number 10 Downing Street, London, Prime Minister Asquith was angrily pacing back and forth, livid as he finished reading a communiqué while Kitchener waited next to his desk.

Asquith finished reading, looked up, and yelled, "Not even a bloody tugboat?! I ordered the escort *doubled!* She's a sitting duck! Where were you on this?! I want that bastard Churchill in here right now!"

"I'm afraid that's impossible, Prime Minister," Kitchener said. "He's in Paris at the moment."

"Oh that's just bloody great! And any hope we had of winning this war will soon be at the bottom of the sea!"

He balled the communiqué up and hurled it at the wall.

* * *

Inside the *U-20*, the quiet submarine was bathed in a pulsing, soft, red glow.

Captain Schwieger's eyes were glued to the periscope. In his crosshairs: the RMS *Lusitania*.

"Torpedo armed," Torpedo Officer Wiesbach said softly.

"Stand by to fire," Schwieger replied calmly. "On my signal."

Schwieger watched and waited. And watched and waited.

He muttered to himself, "*Schmitt, komm schon, mann. Wo . . . ist . . . meine . . . verdammte . . . signalisieren . . .*" (Schmitt, come on, man. Where . . . is . . . my . . . damn . . . signal . . .)

CHAPTER 21

BETRAYED

In the forward cargo hold of the *Lusitania*, Schmitt was scanning the empty ocean with his binoculars. He saw no ships, no movement, no ripples or bubbles, not even a whale, all the way to the horizon. He refocused, scanned back across the panorama . . . stopped suddenly as he spotted a tiny glint of reflected sunlight just above the waterline.

He smiled, put down the glasses, and turned to his captives.

"Don't you find it strange," he said to Cornwell, "that here we are, in waters known to be teeming with certain armed fish of German persuasion, and no one is coming to your rescue?"

He jabbed a finger upward, saying, "And above in this very ship, your captain is meandering along at, what, ten knots; he's not zigzagging at all—why it almost seems as if he wants to go down! Perhaps he's a German saboteur too—my fellow spy!"

Cornwell's jaw clenched. Tesla and Li looked on, helpless, guarded by three machine-gun-toting Germans.

Schmitt wagged a scolding finger at Cornwell and continued his diatribe.

"Once again your Winston Churchill disappoints. He was warned to expect additional submarines. Did he not pass the warnings on to the Royal Navy so they could protect merchant vessels? I think not. Yet, your own battleship, *Orion*, was held back from these waters on her return from Devonport to Scotland until three days ago—and even then she was ordered to stay one hundred miles from the Irish coast! Ha! And how do I know all this, you might wonder? I'm an officer in US Army Intelligence! HA!"

He guffawed and slapped his thigh in glee, then drilled Cornwell with a hard look.

"Just like at Gallipoli, when that boob Fisher and that moron Churchill gummed up the works and foot soldiers were left to die in the mud."

"Not without putting up a bloody good fight, to be sure!" Cornwell snapped.

Schmitt's jaw dropped in mock shock. He looked at the others, saying, "Do you believe the flaccid arrogance of this buffoon?"

Suddenly, Cornwell spun around—free of his bonds—grabbed the guard nearest him and jammed Tesla's lightning bolt cigarette lighter into his neck—a blue-white arc of electricity sizzled into him like a cutting torch, filling the air with the smell of charred flesh. The guard screamed, grabbed at the burning hole below his chin—Cornwell used him as a shield and fired the stunned guard's machine gun at one of the other guards, riddling him with slugs.

Tesla and Li dove for cover—Schmitt reeled, scooped the gun from his holster, and squeezed the trigger—a line of hot lead from his Mauser stitched across the crates, raking a trail of sparks along the steel walls as he tried to duck out of the way of Cornwell's deadly machine gun fire.

* * *

A few hundred meters away and just a few feet below the surface of the ocean, Captain Walther Schwieger's *U-20* had the *Lusitania* square in the crosshairs and was bearing down on her like a shark on a seal.

"Target acquired," Schwieger said to Torpedo Officer Wiesbach. "Range, 900 meters. Set running depth at three meters."

"Aye, Captain."

As he watched the *Lusitania* grow larger in his periscope, Schwieger saw erratic pops of light coming from the open door of the luxury liner's forward cargo hold. He pressed his face closer to the viewfinder. He smiled.

"We have the signal. Time?"

Wiesbach looked at his watch and said, "14:10, sir."

"Prepare to fire."

"Ready to fire."

* * *

In the *Lusitania* cargo hold, Cornwell, face hard, eyes fixed, sliced the guard to ribbons firing the machine gun. He swept his aim around—bullets hit the third armed guard in the head—Schmitt twice in the shoulder—Schmitt continued firing as he fell to the floor, his shots slamming into Claire's side, spinning her around to fall on top of Schmitt at the base of the pulse weapon.

The firefight ended almost as quickly as it had begun. The smell of fresh blood and burned flesh hung in the still, quiet air.

Tesla and Li rose slowly, surveying the carnage.

Clutching the smoking machine gun by the barrel and the handle, Cornwell's eyes took a swift, professional assessment of the bodies as he swung around in a circle, counting to himself.

"Guard one . . . the woman . . . Schmitt . . . guard two . . . guard three."

He dropped the barrel, held the gun by the grip, and let out a breath, muttering, "That should do it."

Li rushed to Claire, rolled her off Schmitt's body, put his head to her chest, and listened for her heartbeat.

"She's alive!" he exclaimed.

"She's a spy, too, I'm afraid," Cornwell said, treading over to them. "And she was more than willing to watch you die not ten minutes ago." Standing over her and Li, he raised the machine gun at her. He pulled back the rack, taking aim at Claire.

Li threw himself over her body, looked up at Cornwell hovering over them, and cried out, "You can't just murder her! You're not judge and jury!"

"In wartime situations like these . . . I'm afraid I am judge and jury, my friend. Now move aside. She's a traitor and a spy."

"Stop!" Tesla yelled. "This ends—*now!*"

Cornwell looked up at Tesla who was walking toward the open hold door facing the sea, holding the core like a baseball he was ready to throw.

"Now, Nikola, wait. Hear me out," Cornwell said firmly. "If we don't use this weapon on the German submarine that is waiting out there right now—the sub Schmitt signaled, the one he said was coming to take your pulse weapon to Germany—everyone on this ship will perish."

Tesla stopped and looked out at the ocean. He turned to look at the pulse weapon, his eyes pausing as they swept over Li and Claire.

"Don't kill her," he said to Cornwell. "If you must do something, then let a military tribunal or whatever it is your sort do, take care of it. Are we agreed?"

Cornwell glanced down at Claire. Li was cradling her head in his lap, his face a mixture of fear and determination as he looked up at Cornwell's gun.

Cornwell lowered the gun, nodded, and said, "Agreed."

Tesla walked over to the pulse weapon and opened the breech.

* * *

That same instant, just a few meters beneath the waves, the *U-20* was steadily advancing on the *Lusitania*. The sub's torpedo hatch slid open.

Inside, Schwieger was glued to the periscope viewfinder, his emotionless voice preparing his crew for mass slaughter.

"Range."

"Eight hundred meters . . . 755 . . . 750 . . ."

"Fire in five . . . four . . ."

* * *

In the cargo hold, as the pulse weapon powered up, a low-level humming sound began to emanate from the device, the sound bouncing off the steel walls and filling the room with rumbling pressure waves.

Cornwell said to Tesla, "I'm going to have to pull rank on you, Dr. Tesla. It's probably best that this one be on me, as the officer on deck." He stepped to Tesla's side. "Where's the trigger?"

Tesla pointed to a dial on the side of the device. "Right here. It's a power capacitor. Like a variable flow regulator. Clockwise to add power. Counterclockwise to power back. Better let me dial the power flow so you can aim it."

"Right," Cornwell said, taking over control of the weapon.

He put his eye to the sight, searching the sea outside the hull door. He swept around in a small arc looking for the submarine.

"Now . . . where is the little bugger," he mumbled as he scanned the surface of the ocean.

He panned more slowly back the other direction . . . stopped . . . moved the opposite way a tiny bit.

"Gotcha!" he said as he spotted the tall, thin periscope headed directly at them. "Get ready, Nikola! When I say fire."

Tesla nervously rested his fingers on the dial and said unsteadily, "Ready when you are, I guess . . . not really used to this killing business."

Cornwell glanced at Tesla, then back to the sight.

"You sure you got this, Nicky?"

Tesla brushed his hand on his trousers and started to answer, when Li's hand suddenly reached in and gripped the dial.

"I've got it," Li said, stepping in front of Tesla.

Tesla backed away and gave Li a grateful look.

Cornwell nodded and smiled, his eye never leaving the sight. "Good man, Li." He aimed the weapon lower, pointing just beneath the surface of the water, below the periscope, and said, "Ready on my call."

"Ready when you are," Li said, looking out at the approaching periscope as the sub moved toward them at attack speed.

* * *

"Fire!" Captain Schwieger called out in the control room of the *U-20*.

"Torpedo away!" Wiesbach responded.

With a speeding whoosh of air and bubbles, a gyroscope torpedo cut loose from its tube and sped toward its hapless victim.

* * *

"Fire!" yelled Cornwell in the cargo hold of the *Lusitania*.

Li cranked the dial full clockwise . . . the high-pitched humming became a deafening roar as the super weapon let loose its pulse.

At the bow of the *Lusitania*, a lookout saw the deadly thin line of churning water hurtling toward the ship.

"Torpedo!" he screamed. "Torpedo!"

At that same moment, a lookout, high up in the liner's crow's nest, also spied the deadly wake flying at the ship.

"Starboard side!" he yelled, climbing out of the basket and scrambling down the mast ladder. "Torpedo coming!"

CHAPTER 22

Showdown

The torpedo slammed into the *Lusitania*'s starboard side, just below the bridge. Metal plates on the underside of the hull flexed on impact as the underwater missile pierced through. Then, the torpedo detonated, sending a shower of steel plating, debris, coal, dust, and water upward, rocking the ship like a toy boat in a bathtub. One of her funnels buckled. A steam boiler was sent hundreds of feet into the sky.

Down below, the forward cargo hold was violently jolted as water and metal exploded outside the open door. Cornwell was thrown back from the pulse weapon but held fast his aim on the submarine.

Up on the bridge, Captain Turner shouted orders.

“Quartermaster! Hard starboard for the coast!”

“Aye, sir!”

“Damage report?!”

The executive officer looked at the captain and said, “It’s bad, sir. Probably mortal. Listing to starboard. Taking on water fast.”

“Tend to the passengers! Women and children first—you know the drill!”

“Yes, sir.”

The executive officer left the bridge in a rush.

The quartermaster said, “Captain, she’s not responding to the wheel—we can’t hold course.”

“Reverse all engines and make sure the radio room sent the SOS. Position: sixteen kilometers south, Old Head of Kinsale. Quickly, quartermaster!—before we lose power!”

“Aye, sir!”

Down in the hold, as Cornwell was holding fast to the super weapon aimed at the submarine, several gunshots suddenly rang out, hitting Cornwell again and again.

Tesla and Li spun around just as Cornwell slumped dead over the weapon—behind them . . . stood the ever-resilient Claire LeFleur, with Schmitt’s smoking Mauser in her little hand, aimed straight at them.

“Both of you!” she ordered them as she helped Schmitt to his feet, “Stay back!”

Schmitt stood, his adrenaline pumping, shoulder a hamburgered mess, eyes seething rage, and blood seeping from his wounds. He staggered to the weapon, shoved Cornwell’s body off, and kick rolled it to the door while Claire held Tesla and Li at bay.

Schmitt dialed the power back and shoved the aim of the weapon upward and away from the *U-20*, which was slowly surfacing 300 yards away and closing.

Schmitt turned to Tesla, breathing hard, bloody hand clutching his upper arm, and said, "You are going to help me load this thing onto the U-boat." He threw a glance at Claire and added, "Or this little creampuff here—probably the first woman your Chinaman ever had—will paint the hull with your brains."

"Claire," Li said, his eyes imploring, barely masking his love, hurt, longing, and sorrow. "Would your father be proud?"

Schmitt turned to Claire. Her eyes were locked on Li's, both hands gripping the Mauser.

"Stop!" she said, raising the pistol.

"Did you even have a father who served as a general in China?" Li continued. "Was that a lie, too?"

"Li, please!" she pleaded, aiming the gun at him with shaky hands.

"*Please?*" Schmitt said to her condescendingly. "He's a mongrel. You're above that."

"You're the first woman I ever loved," Li said to her.

"No more!" she cried out in a quivering, pained voice, pulling back the hammer.

Schmitt smiled, looked at Li, and said, "See what you missed, Nicky. A tough woman. German at heart. Not such a creampuff after all, eh? Does what she's told, goes where she's ordered." He turned to her and said, "Shoot him. *Now.* I don't need him."

Claire spun the gun, aimed it at Schmitt—cried out, "But *I* do!"

BOOM! Schmitt held there for a brief moment, confusion on his face as he looked down at his chest for the bullet hole—then they heard another BOOM!

But they weren't gunshots—it was the *Lusitania*, grinding beneath them as the great ship struggled against breaking up and being pulled down by the ocean.

The ship slammed to a jarring stop, shoving them all off balance—Schmitt threw himself on the pulse weapon, spinning the barrel into Claire—the muzzle caught her, lifted her entire body up, pinned her to the doorjamb, leaving her legs dangling precariously over the sea and her arms clutching the barrel of the weapon. Her crushed lungs gasped for breath; only the pulse weapon kept her from falling into the ocean—which was quickly rising up the hull as the ship began to sink.

Li leapt toward Schmitt—but Schmitt was already scooping the Mauser from Claire's weakened grasp—he spun back—Li reached him only to have Schmitt point the gun at his forehead right between his eyes.

Li stopped and remained very still; he was locked eye to eye with Schmitt. He glanced at Claire. She was coughing crimson, weakened by excruciating pain. Her hands trembled as they hugged the barrel and the light was slowly draining from her eyes.

Li's eyes suddenly widened as he looked at Claire. Schmitt turned to follow his gaze—Claire's shaking hand was reaching for the breech—Schmitt swung his gun around—aimed at her—pulled the trigger. *Click!*

Nothing.

Click. Click.

Li leapt at Schmitt just as Schmitt lunged at Claire—Schmitt got a finger on the weapon's power dial, shoving it all the way clockwise just as Li smashed him aside with an elbow to the head and reached out to Claire.

"No!" Tesla cried, leaping out and grabbing Li by the collar just as a white-hot bolt of lightning engulfed Claire.

Tesla, Li, and Schmitt stood there, watching helplessly as Claire's body began to vibrate rapidly. They looked on in horror as she started to disintegrate into flashes of electric light and rainbow vapor, her face painfully aware of what was happening to her, her eyes pleading as they looked at Li.

"*NOOO!!*" Li cried, fighting against the blinding waves of light and particles flitting around her, in her, through her.

Li reached for her outstretched hand. At the instant their fingers would have touched, her hand dissolved into mist that began moving up her arm, her shoulder, and finally overtaking her entire body, converting her to sparkling bits of pure light.

As Li looked into her face, the fear began melting from her eyes. She smiled serenely. Her peaceful, contented gaze was no longer looking at him . . . but through him, to something beyond him. And then . . . she dissolved into a million shimmering fragments.

And she was gone.

Tesla reached out to dial the weapon off.

Schmitt threw his arm up and cried out in awe, "Germany will rule the world!—the universe!"

Li flew at Schmitt in a rage, leaping onto him with fury, slamming him to the floor, knocking the Mauser away, and pounding mercilessly on the bigger man.

Using raw, brute strength, Schmitt heaved himself to his feet, grabbed Li by the throat, and hurled him against the weapon.

Li looked down at the Mauser, resting halfway between them. Schmitt made a dive for the pistol. Li's foot swept out and kicked the gun away from Schmitt's fingers. Li followed through with a spinning kick at Schmitt that crashed into Schmitt's jaw and sent him sprawling against the steel bulkhead wall with a hard thud.

Schmitt rolled away as Li advanced. He shook it off, sprang to his feet, shouting, "You only get one of those, you yellow dog. Let's finish this!"

Schmitt took a southpaw boxer's stance, his one good arm up, the other dangled by his side, blood flowing profusely and pooling on the floor.

Li shook his arms out, danced around on the balls of his feet, easily ducking Schmitt's jabs, and smiled.

"I've never taken pleasure in hurting anyone, but I will enjoy killing you, Schmitt."

Tesla looked down, put a hand on his forehead, and said, "Oh, God. Here it comes."

"Then it's to the death, chink. Now, come on—fight like a man!" Schmitt bellowed.

"Find me a man to fight and I will," Li grinned and did a fast foot shuffle. "*Whaaa!*"

Schmitt charged, throwing right hook after right hook pummeling Li furiously. Li responded with a display of dexterity that made Schmitt look like he was standing still.

As they fought, Tesla was attempting to get the core out of the weapon's breech but was thwarted at every try by Schmitt or Li as they thrashed about, kicking and beating each other.

Gradually, Li gained the upper hand as Schmitt's strength ebbed from all the blood he was losing. Li knocked Schmitt against the body of a dead guard. Schmitt spied a knife sheathed at the dead man's waist. He grabbed it, rolled onto his back, slipped it behind his own belt as he moved, and leapt up with a raised fist just in time to meet Li's furious attack. Schmitt grappled with Li—wrapped a burly arm around him—pulled the knife out with his weakened left hand—and stabbed him again and again.

Li rolled, ducked, weaved; yet, he couldn't break the bear hold . . . took the repeated stabs . . . and fell limp to the floor.

Tesla started toward Li. Schmitt stepped between them, brandishing the knife. They both eyed the Mauser halfway between them. Tesla made a fake move. Schmitt tossed the knife and ran for the gun. Tesla ignored it, rushed to Li, took off his jacket, and jammed it to Li's stomach to staunch the blood flow.

Schmitt turned, grimacing in pain, glaring at Tesla. He aimed the gun at him.

"Shoot me if you like," Tesla stated calmly as he tended to Li's wounds. "But I will not be used to help you carry out your madness."

"Oh, you will definitely help. And so will they," Schmitt responded, looking out the hull door at the *U-20* a hundred yards away. He pulled back the hammer on the pistol, aimed at it Tesla, and added, "Now get up. We have work to finish before this tub goes under."

"What are you going to do, shoot me?" Tesla said, not even looking at Schmitt. "Do that and you'll never have another one of those." He jerked his head in the direction of the weapon near the door, adding, "I'm afraid your super weapon is going down with the ship. Just like all of us."

Schmitt looked at the pulse weapon: the muzzle was wedged solidly against the metal doorjamb. He tried to muscle it free with his one good arm. It wouldn't budge. He opened the breech—he abruptly flinched backward at the sight of the blue-white lightning pulsating in the core.

Schmitt said, "Good. At least the important part is still working. You'll build another one for the motherland. You'll grow to love Germany, with time. You'll have Germany's finest scientists under your command. And I'll have you under mine."

Schmitt ejected the core from the weapon, held the brightly sparkling power source up to the open door, and waved it once in the direction of the *U-20*. Then twice.

* * *

On the deck of the surfaced *U-20*, Wiesbach was manning the forward deck gun and Schwieger was looking through his binoculars at the crippled and sinking *Lusitania*, her bow dipping on the starboard side, black smoke pouring from the hole where the boiler had blasted through. Crewmen were trying to get the collapsible lifeboats ready, and throngs of passengers fought to crowd into the fixed lifeboats and get off the ship before she went down.

As he peered at the open cargo bay door, Schwieger muttered anxiously, "Hurry, Schmitt, hurry, man."

He saw a light flash from the open bay. Then a second one.

"Something has gone wrong," he said.

He glanced at Wiesbach, saying, "Tell the engine room half speed ahead, Mr. Wiesbach. Put a man on the aft deck gun and have them launch the fast boat. This is now a rescue. I don't want my sailors out there alone."

"Aye, Captain."

* * *

At the *Lusitania*'s cargo hold door, Schmitt waved the core one more time. He turned back to the hold just as Tesla was dragging Li out the bulkhead door and into the corridor.

Schmitt yelled out and cut loose with the Mauser on full auto, digging a line of divots in the steel walls. But he was too late. Tesla pulled Li to safety around the corner and fell to the floor as the last slugs sparked and ricocheted across the corridor just inches from where they lay.

Schmitt stomped toward them and stumbled as the ship suddenly shifted and let out a great wrenching sound of tearing steel plates giving way. The ship shuddered and pulled herself down deeper into the water. The sudden movement of the ship dislodged the weapon, and it fell into the water, sinking instantly.

Schmitt caught his balance and looked out through the smoke at the *U-20*'s fast boat heading toward him. One of the armed crewmembers flashed a signal light. Schmitt waved the core in response. The *Lusitania* abruptly shifted again. The waves were now lapping at Schmitt's feet and the cargo bay door sank ever closer to the ocean. Crates and cargo slid and tumbled with loud crashes, blocking the door where Tesla and Li had escaped seconds ago.

Outside in the corridor, Tesla shielded Li as a crate slammed into the doorway and lodged itself fast. Li's eyes fluttered weakly.

Tesla removed his blood-soaked jacket from Li's stomach and inspected the wounds.

Their eyes met. Tesla forced a smile.

"Eh. Not as bad as I thought," he lied.

Tesla took off his shirt to pack it around Li's wounds. He looked nervously down the smoke-filled corridor and heard the frightened screams and cries of hundreds of passengers on the decks above as they tried to escape the sinking ship.

He stood, leaned down to Li, scooped an arm around his back, and said, "Come on, old friend. Let's get you to your feet and get out of here. Schmitt is in for the surprise of his short life when that core hits the water. The reaction will be devastating. Okay on three . . ."

He got Li to his feet. They staggered into the smoke.

In the cargo hold, Schmitt tucked the core into the inner pocket of his coat as the fast boat approached outside.

The boat pulled alongside the sinking vessel. Debris from upper decks rained down between Schmitt and the boat. He ducked back inside just as a piece of heavy machinery thundered past from somewhere above him and crashed into the water.

"Now, Major Schmitt!" a crewman yelled and held out a hand. "You'll have to jump, sir! We'll get you!"

Schmitt turned to the door, saying to himself, "History will remember this moment."

He jumped.

CHAPTER 23

SINKING OF THE *LUSITANIA*

Schmitt splashed into the cold water, feet first, dwarfed by the hull of the massive ocean liner.

The fast boat swiftly motored to where he had gone under and waited for him to emerge.

Two seconds passed. Five. Ten.

"Where is he?!" the skipper called out to the other crewmen. "Do you see him?!"

"*Nien*!"

They frantically looked around for Schmitt.

Twenty more seconds. Thirty.

The skipper dove into the water and swam downward in search of Schmitt.

He found Schmitt five feet beneath the boat, writhing in agony, his chest glowing white, his face contorted hideously as he fought to keep his mouth closed, trying to claw his way upward. But he was stuck in place. His eyes held an expression of sheer agony as they stared unseeingly at the skipper. The skipper swam to him—stopped as Schmitt's mouth suddenly gaped open in a horrific silent scream, his chest swelled up, and smoke-filled bubbles burst from inside him.

The skipper turned, swimming quickly upward to the boat, his hands and feet fighting furiously to get away from what was to come.

Underwater, the core suddenly exploded. Schmitt's body vaporized into a huge mist of bloody chum, forcing the skipper high out of the water just as his hands had grabbed the edge of the inflatable fast boat.

The explosion crackled through the armaments and firearms stored in the hold of the ship, setting off another devastating detonation that lifted the entire mighty ship upward a few feet and ripped a whale-sized gash in her double-hulled bottom.

The *Lusitania* slammed hard back down on the waves, listing even more severely to the starboard. Water gushed into the ship.

As Tesla and Li struggled down the smoke-filled corridor, the sudden explosion hurled them against the wall like rag dolls. Tesla caught his breath, leaned down to Li, reached under his arm, and tried to help the gravely wounded Li to his feet.

"Come on, old boy," Twain's voice said encouragingly. "You're almost there."

Tesla looked up, giving a faint smile to his old friend, whose white hair, white jacket, and white pants stood out like an angelic beacon in the dust-filled, smoky corridor.

Tesla heaved with all his strength, got Li's arm around his shoulder, pulled Li to his feet, and they continued fighting their way through the throng of hundreds of third-class passengers to the packed and smoke-filled stairwell that led topside.

Twain led the way, cane held aloft, saying calmly to the onslaught of rushing, fear-ridden passengers, "Step aside, please. Thank you. All will be fine. Don't panic."

It had been several minutes since the *U-20* torpedo had slammed into the *Lusitania*. The ship's speed had reduced enough so her crew could begin lowering lifeboats. The ship was listing so far to starboard that the boats were too far away from the hull for passengers to safely board them. The port side was now beginning to lean more horizontal than vertical, and lifeboats being lowered were dragging along the bull and snagging on the rivets, damaging the wooden boats as they scraped their way toward the water, and adding to the din and cacophony of the death throes of a once-magnificent ship.

Lifeboats overturned and passengers tumbled into the choppy ocean. Other lifeboats crashed down onto the deck, hitting passengers, knocking some overboard. There were forty-eight lifeboats—enough for all passengers to safely escape the carnage . . . yet only half a dozen, all on the starboard side, made it safely to the water.

Many people had no choice but to leap and swim for it.

On the top deck, the scene was a whirlwind of flying debris, screaming panic, and tearful despair as the ship was being dragged downward.

Elbert and Alice Hubbard clung to the railing. A steward offered the couple life jackets.

Hubbard smiled gamely, lightly joked to the man, "You go help others, young man. Mrs. Hubbard isn't quite finished with her cake—and believe me, you don't want to find yourself between her and her dessert. We'll be fine."

Just then, Tesla and Li staggered onto the badly sloping deck—Tesla quickly swung Li aside as a lifeboat filled with screaming passengers clinging to one another, careened down the tilted deck. Tesla watched helplessly as terrified people were bowled over and crushed by the boat as it crashed into the railing and plunged into the water.

Tesla caught his breath, looking around the horrific, mesmerizing scene. He spotted Vanderbilt, ushering life-jacketed children into a lifeboat.

Vanderbilt looked up, saw Tesla and Li, and rushed over to them.

"Good Lord, man—is he all right?!"

Tesla shook his head gravely.

Vanderbilt got on the other side of Li, and he and Tesla made their way through the crowd.

"Make way!" Vanderbilt said as they moved slowly into the teeming, panicked throng. "Make way! Injured man here—can we get some help?!"

"Let's just get him into a lifeboat," Tesla said.

"I'll do better than that," Vanderbilt said.

Vanderbilt helped Tesla get Li into a nearly full lifeboat. Just as it was being launched, Vanderbilt suddenly shoved Tesla into the boat too.

"Wha—?!" Tesla yelled, confused. "You can't do this!—what about you? You have so much to offer the world!"

"With what?" Vanderbilt called to Tesla as the lifeboat began descending toward the water below. "Money? I earned none of it and I'd just spend all of it if I lived long enough. A new world is dawning, my dear Tesla! I'm but a remnant of a gilded age. The twentieth century will be created by the vision and inventions of men like you!"

They were now fifty feet apart. Vanderbilt continued helping other passengers as Tesla began to slide slowly from his view.

Tesla called out, "Alfred, jump, you can make it."

"It was my great pleasure to have spent time with the most brilliant man the world has ever known," Vanderbilt shouted cheerfully. "I just make money, but *you* make it a better place. Be off now—I have work to do here!"

With that, Vanderbilt, smiling and helping people as if he had found a new passion in life, faded into the mist and smoke above as Tesla's lifeboat reached the water.

Tesla cradled Li on the floor of the boat, and he caught a glimpse of the last few curved inches of the cold, gray hull of the *U-20* as it slid stealthily beneath the waves . . . and disappeared.

Within minutes, the mighty Greyhound of the Sea, too, slipped under . . . and was no more.

Tesla huddled in the lifeboat amid dozens of other weeping, stunned, tattered passengers, in the sudden strange quiet that had been, just twenty minutes earlier, filled with the sound of sheer, wild fear, explosions, shouting. And death.

He looked down at Li whose breathing was short and labored.

"He'll be with me, soon," Twain said softly from the other side of the boat with his hand poised on his cane; a kind, sad smile on his craggy, wise face; and his eyes fixed on the distant Irish shore.

Tesla hugged Li closely . . . and wept.

"Sleep my friend," he whispered in Li's ear, clutching him tightly. "Sleep. And when you awake, you will be in a world that deeply loves and greatly values men such as you."

Those were the last words Li Yín Huŏ would ever hear on earth.

CHAPTER 24

Tesla's Tale

One afternoon a month after the disaster at sea, Nikola Tesla stood alone in the Woodlawn Cemetery in New York, looking down at a grave. Carved into solid granite beneath the bronze headstone plaque was a simple epitaph:

Samuel Langhorne Clemens—Mark Twain—Nov. 30, 1835–Apr. 21, 1910

Dozens of withered and dried bouquets were packed around the tombstone, along with many more fresh flowers.

In one hand, Tesla held a small green plant. In the other, a ceramic cylinder that was ornately decorated in Chinese symbols, silver-rimmed licks of red-orange fire, and floral patterns.

Tesla looked down at Twain's grave, saying . . .

"So, anyway, my friend . . . that's how Li died," he said softly.

He sniffled, quickly wiped away a tear, and mumbled, "I think I'm catching a cold."

He knelt down, set the plant aside, and scooped several handfuls of earth from around Twain's tombstone. He unscrewed the ceramic cylinder, and reverently poured light, powdery ashes into the freshly dug hole. He looked inside the container, saw that there were still some ashes remaining, and started to shake it out . . . then he stopped. He held the cylinder up to the sunlight and looked at the name, painted in Chinese-like English characters on the front of the cylinder: *Li Yín Huŏ*. He closed his eyes for a moment, his lips moving in silent prayer. Then he put the lid back on the cylinder and set it aside.

He freed the plant from its small pot, leaned down, and placed it in the dirt hole on top of the ashes. He covered the plant and ashes with dirt, and patted the earth down, slowly and precisely.

Then he said, forcing back his emotions, "*Jednog dana, Li Yín Huŏ, ljudska svest će pomeriti granice života i biće nova era mudrosti . . . razumevanje vremena . . . otkriće izvora energije neograničene. Ali najviše od svega, dragi moj Li, neće biti rasizam, bez predrasuda, bez mržnje prelepih ljudi poput tebe.*" (One day, Li Yín Huŏ, human consciousness will shift the boundaries of life and there will be a new era of wisdom . . . the understanding of time . . . the discovery of a source of limitless energy. But most of all, my dear Li, there will be no racism, no prejudice, no hatred of beautiful people like you.)

He finished his soliloquy in a near whisper, fighting a flood of emotions, and cried out plaintively, "*Videćete, prijatelju moj! Videćete*!" (You will see, my friend! You will see!)

Suddenly overcome, he caved forward onto the dirt, embracing the little plant in the crook of one arm, his head on his forearms, sobbing in anguish.

"Li," he sputtered through his tears, "remember that day, many years ago right at this very spot, when you asked me if I was going to miss Twain? Why do I feel like I miss you so very much more?"

He let himself go, his entire body grieving, tears running through his fingers and into the dirt.

After a few moments, he slowly pulled himself to his feet, took a strong breath through his nose, and brushed the dirt off his shirt and pants.

He looked down at the resting place of his two closest friends.

"Now, Twain," he said, wiping his tears with a handkerchief, "please, don't let anyone belittle Li. He did not deserve how people treated him. And make sure people thank him when he helps them—he helped so many people, you know."

He stopped talking and surveyed the manicured green cemetery, glanced up at the blue sky, and closed his eyes. Suddenly, the sound of a police siren broke his peaceful reverie. He opened his eyes and turned to get a view of the cemetery gate. An NYPD squad car was entering the cemetery, followed closely by a brand new Cadillac Phaeton Tourer.

Tesla squatted down, picked up the ceramic cylinder, brushed it off, and slipped it into his pocket. As he stood up, he saw Twain and Li, strolling arm-in-arm across the grass, chatting amiably, heading toward the gate. The cars momentarily blocked Tesla's view of his friends . . . and in the two seconds it took for the vehicles to drive past them, Twain and Li were gone.

Tesla smiled and whispered, "Good-bye, my friends. Take care of one another."

The two vehicles rolled to a stop at the curb fifty feet away. Two men emerged from the backseat of the Cadillac. One was Secretary of War Lindley Miller Garrison. The other wore the uniform of a US Army colonel.

Two police officers got out of the NYPD squad car, lit cigarettes, leaned against the fender of the vehicle, and watched Garrison and the colonel tread up the grassy knoll toward Tesla.

Tesla shook his head, gave a quick last wipe to his face, pocketed his handkerchief, and muttered tersely, "I cannot even begin to imagine what he wants with me this time . . ."

EPILOGUE: THE AFTERMATH

This book is dedicated to the memory of the 1,198 children, women, and men, including 128 American citizens, who lost their lives when *Lusitania* was sunk on May 7, 1915. It took less than eighteen minutes for the majestic ship to sink.

Nikola Tesla, responsible for the invention of alternating current, radio transmission, remote control, and too many other inventions to mention, died on January 7, 1943, in the New Yorker Hotel, penniless and alone.

In a coroner's inquiry on May 10, 1915, Captain Turner admitted that he had received warnings about submarines and stated that he had carried out other orders and instructions from the Admiralty that he was not allowed to discuss. Thirty minutes after a coroner's inquest concluded, the crown solicitor for County Cork, Ireland, appeared with instructions that Captain Turner was barred from giving evidence and was not allowed to make any further statements about instructions he may or may not have been given concerning shipping, submarines, deviations from standing operating orders, or the cargo manifest of the *Lusitania*.

At subsequent hearings, Captain Turner, Cunard, and the Royal Navy were absolved of all negligence, and blame for the disaster was laid at the feet of the government of Germany.

On November 16, 2014, the United States Navy tested a laser pulse weapon. It is due to be deployed in 2017.

We have not heard the last of Nikola Tesla for, as his unique and brilliant inventions are being increasingly rediscovered and revived one after another around the world, he still has many new stories to tell.

Acknowledgments

I would like to thank Michael Rutledge McCall, a great developmental editor. I would also like to thank several people for their participation this project. Lisa, without your support and understanding this would have been much more difficult than it was. Joan, Kent, Markus T, Paul, Jim, Chad, Michael and Dale, your help in this endeavor is very much appreciated. I would also like to thank Jerrold Jenkins for his guidance.

About the Author

Ronald J. Walters has always been captivated by the *Lusitania* and the fact that its place in history has been obscured by the *Titanic's* sinking. He researched everything available on the *Lusitania* for over three years and, with the 100th anniversary taking place in 2015, decided to write a screenplay that is fact-based, but with an entertaining twist that could offer answers to some of the lingering questions surrounding the conspiracy. After several productive meetings in Hollywood, Walters found himself on the Paramount lot, when a film executive asked, "So, when is the book coming out?" From that conversation, this book was born. Walters lives in Traverse City, Michigan, where he enjoys working on his golf game.